Grave
Matters

Patricia H. Rushford

Books by Patricia Rushford

Young Adult Fiction

JENNIE McGRADY MYSTERIES

1. *Too Many Secrets*
2. *Silent Witness*
3. *Pursued*
4. *Deceived*
5. *Without a Trace*
6. *Dying to Win*
7. *Betrayed*
8. *In Too Deep*
9. *Over the Edge*
10. *From the Ashes*
11. *Desperate Measures*
12. *Abandoned*
13. *Forgotten*
14. *Stranded*
15. *Grave Matters*

Adult Fiction

Morningsong

HELEN BRADLEY MYSTERIES

1. *Now I Lay Me Down to Sleep*
2. *Red Sky in Mourning*
3. *A Haunting Refrain*
4. *When Shadows Fall*

Grave Matters

Patricia H. Rushford

GRACE BRETHREN CHURCH
13000 ZEKIAH DRIVE
WALDORF, MARYLAND 20601

BETHANY HOUSE PUBLISHERS
MINNEAPOLIS, MINNESOTA 55438

#3511

Grave Matters
Copyright © 2002
Patricia H. Rushford

Cover illustration by Sergio Giovine
Cover design by Lookout Design Group, Inc.

ISBN 0-7642-2123-X

Published by Bethany House Publishers
A Ministry of Bethany Fellowship International
11400 Hampshire Avenue South
Bloomington, Minnesota 55438
www.bethanyhouse.com

Printed in the United States of America by
Bethany Press International
Bloomington, Minnesota 55438

To all the kids and grown-ups who have remained
faithful Jennie McGrady fans all these years.
Jennie is retiring—for a while, at least—and I know you'll
share in the disappointment of seeing the series end.

Thank you.

PATRICIA RUSHFORD is an award-winning writer, speaker, and teacher who has published numerous articles and more than thirty-five books, including *What Kids Need Most in a Mom* and *Have You Hugged Your Teenager Today?*, as well as the JENNIE MCGRADY MYSTERIES. She is a registered nurse and has a master's degree in counseling from Western Evangelical Seminary. She and her husband, Ron, live in Washington State and have two grown children, seven grandchildren, and lots of nephews and nieces.

Pat has been reading mysteries for as long as she can remember. She is a member of Mystery Writers of America and several other writing organizations. She is also the co-director of Writer's Weekend at the Beach and teaches at writers' conferences and schools across the country.

1

"Jennie!" Mom called up from the landing on the first floor. "Gram's here."

"Be right down." Jennie McGrady flipped her long, dark hair back and looked in the mirror one last time. Gram had said to dress comfortably, so she'd put on her favorite jeans and blue sweater over a white blouse. Because May weather could be unpredictable, Jennie had gone for the layered look. She adjusted the collar and frowned. "Do you think this looks okay?"

"It's fine. You look gorgeous." Lisa Calhoun, Jennie's cousin and best friend, hung her head over the end of Jennie's bed and brushed the rats out of her curls. She'd stayed overnight as it was the last they'd see of each other for two, maybe three, weeks. "Everything looks good on you."

Jennie rolled her eyes. "Hardly." She wasn't gorgeous, not like Lisa, who had red hair, green eyes, and a figure to die for. Jennie was tall and thin. She did have nice eyes, though—dark blue, like her father's and Gram's.

"You sound as nervous as Gram."

"What are you talking about?" Jennie leaned down to pick up her pajamas and toss them in the hamper.

"Last night at our house—didn't you notice? She looked more like she was going to war than to a family reunion in Ireland."

Jennie shrugged. "She seemed okay to me."

"You were probably too excited about the trip to notice. I bet she has an assignment. Maybe with the FBI or something."

Jennie's stomach tightened at the thought. Gram had a knack for getting involved in criminal investigations. She'd been a homicide detective before she retired and took up travel writing. She'd also worked as an undercover agent for the government from time to time. "She's retired from all that, remember? Besides, if she was working on a dangerous assignment, she wouldn't take me with her."

"Hmm. You have a point, but something sure is wrong." Lisa rolled over and sat up, her hair sticking out at all angles.

Is Lisa right? Is Gram working undercover for the government again? Three months earlier, Gram had invited Jennie to go with her to Ireland. Gram would be writing a series of travel articles, and they'd be visiting family and friends. During the last week of their visit, Jennie's mom, dad, and little brother would fly over for a big reunion. The trip was a birthday present from Gram—Jennie would be celebrating her seventeenth birthday there.

"You are so-o-o incredibly lucky," Lisa grumped.

Jennie sat on the bed to put on her sneakers. She *was* lucky. But nervous too. Ireland was an entire continent and an ocean away from Portland, Oregon. She'd never traveled that far in her life. Well, she had when she was small but didn't remember that far back. Could Gram be feeling the same kind of apprehension? Jennie doubted it. Gram traveled way too much to be nervous about it.

"I wish you could come," Jennie said to Lisa.

Lisa shrugged. "Yeah, me too, but Mom doesn't want me to miss school."

"I'm not exactly missing school either, remember? I have to do a genealogy report and a paper on Ireland." Since Jennie was part homeschooled, she had a lot more flexibility than most kids and loved it. "Did you ask your mom and dad about coming later with my parents and Nick?"

As if on cue, Jennie's five-year-old brother tore into the room and came at her like a torpedo. "I don't want you to go, Jennie." He gripped her legs so tight she couldn't move. Nick looked up at her, his big blue eyes fluid with new tears. "Please stay home with us. Gram can go by herself."

Jennie scooped him up. "Come on, Nick. Don't cry. I'll only be gone for two weeks, and then you and Mom and Dad will come to Ireland too. You'll get to fly in a big airplane."

He wriggled down, spread out his arms, and buzzed around the room making zooming airplane sounds.

After half a dozen turns, Jennie scooped Nick up, hugged him, and then dropped him on the bed next to Lisa.

"Hey, Nick. Did you forget? You get to come stay with us this week." Lisa tickled him until he dove off the bed and ran out of the room.

"So are you coming to Ireland with my folks?" Jennie took a deep breath and looked around her room, trying to remember if she'd forgotten anything. Lisa's sleeping bag lay in a heap at the end of the bed.

Lisa rolled off the bed. "I don't know yet. Mom is still thinking about it."

"Well, remind her that we'll be celebrating my birthday over there."

"Oh, right. Like turning seventeen is such a big deal."

"You'd better decide soon or all the flights will be booked."

"I'm not worried." Lisa grabbed her bag out of the closet and pulled out her jeans. "My dad has connections, remember?"

Lisa's dad did have connections. He was an airline pilot. "There still has to be an opening."

"Don't worry."

The way Lisa was acting, so nonchalant and all, Jennie wondered if her cousin was being completely honest. She suspected Lisa had already made plans to fly to Ireland and wanted to surprise her.

"Jennie!" This time it was Gram. "We have to go."

Jennie grabbed her paperback off the bedside table and stuffed it into her bag. "Coming." She rushed out and bounded down the stairs, nearly colliding with Gram at the bottom.

"I'm ready." Jennie swung her bag over her shoulder and leaned over to retie a shoelace. She could hardly wait to get started; at the same time, she already missed her family.

Everyone gathered around Jennie and Gram, hugging them and saying their good-byes. Out on the porch, Dad slipped an arm around Jennie's shoulders. "Think you can manage to stay out of trouble this trip?" The twinkle in his eyes said he was teasing, but his question had a serious side as well. Jennie's curious nature had gotten her into trouble more than once.

"We're just visiting family, Jason." Gram kissed her son's cheek. "Don't worry. She'll be with me. What can go wrong?" She winced at her own words and then laughed. "We'll be fine. I'll take care of her."

Jennie eyed Gram, looking for some clue as to what she might be up to. Gram's gaze met hers, but only for an instant. Lisa was right. Gram did look anxious.

J.B., Gram's husband of nearly a year, picked up the last of Jennie's luggage and followed them to the car. While he stowed the suitcases in the trunk, Jennie climbed into the backseat of the Cadillac and buckled herself in.

Within a few minutes they were heading north on the I-205 toward Portland International Airport. J.B. reached for Gram's hand and in his deep Irish accent said, "It'll be fine, luv. You'll see."

"I know." Gram sighed.

Jennie had no idea what they were talking about and

wasn't certain she should ask. They both sounded strained. The hair on the back of her neck rose and sent a shiver through her. Whatever Gram was up to, J.B. seemed to know about it, which might or might not be a good thing. J.B. had been a government agent before he retired too. In fact, he'd been Gram's boss before they got married. Was he sending her out on a job? Could she be going to Ireland to spy on someone or to help bring down a drug dealer or. . . ?

Don't be ridiculous, McGrady. Jennie scolded herself for letting her imagination take off on a tangent like that. *You're going to visit relatives. End of story.*

So why is Gram acting so weird?

Gram seemed to put whatever was bothering her aside as she smiled and turned back to Jennie. "Are you ready to meet your Irish cousins, darling?"

Jennie swallowed back an unexplained lump in her throat. *Ready for what?* she wanted to ask but didn't. "Sure."

"We'll soon be in Ireland. It hardly seems possible." Gram turned back to J.B.

"And isn't it a grand place, now." J.B. spoke with an even heavier accent than usual. "Once you visit the Emerald Isle, ye'll not be wanting to leave." An odd look passed between him and Gram, and once again Jennie wondered what was going on.

The moment passed. He chuckled and winked at Jennie in the rearview mirror. "Be sure'n catch yourself a leprechaun, now, won't ye, lass?"

"That we will." Jennie followed his lead on the accent.

An hour later, as they were about to go through airport security, J.B. reached into his jacket pocket and pulled out a letter. Handing it to Gram, he said, "This came for you yesterday, luv. Forgot to give it to you."

"Thanks." Gram gave it a cursory glance before slipping it into the pocket of her carryon. "We'll open it later—on the plane."

"Take care, then, luv. You too, Jennie." J.B. hugged Jennie and then reached for Gram. He kissed her long and hard—like he might be worried he wouldn't see her again.

Get real, Jennie told herself. *They're just two ordinary people kissing each other good-bye.*

As Jennie boarded the plane a while later, excitement coursed through her again, causing a little shudder. She shook it off as she had before. *Like Gram told Dad, we're only visiting family. What could go wrong?*

2

If you value your life, stay out of Ireland.

Jennie felt as if she'd been punched in the stomach. Her heart hammered as she folded the threatening note and stuffed it back in the envelope.

What do I do now? She swallowed hard and tucked the note back into the pocket of Gram's carryon. Curiosity had spurred her to open the letter even though it had been addressed to Gram.

You should tell her, Jennie's inner voice answered. She glanced over at her grandmother, who had fallen asleep.

How can I? While Gram might not be intimidated, she'd never allow Jennie to stay in Ireland if there was even a hint of danger. And this was a lot more than a hint. Someone didn't want Gram in Ireland. Well, it was too late now. The plane would be landing at Shannon Airport in less than an hour.

Jennie tugged at her long ponytail, pulling the hair band tighter against her head. *You shouldn't have opened the letter in the first place.* She'd been looking in Gram's bag for a mint, and the letter had fallen out. She wouldn't have opened it at all if it hadn't been from Ireland and if Gram hadn't shared her Ireland letters with the family whenever she received them. The letters were all from Gram's aunt Catherine, who lived on the western coast of Ireland. Auntie, as Gram called her, was faithful about bringing

13

them up-to-date on their Irish cousins, two of whom were close to Jennie's age. And since they'd be staying with those cousins for the next month, Jennie was eager for news about them.

Besides, when J.B. had handed the note to Gram at the airport in Portland, Gram had brushed it aside and tucked it into the side pocket of her carryon. "*We'll* open it later," she'd said, including Jennie. So opening it seemed the logical thing to do.

You have to tell Gram.

"I know, I know," Jennie murmured. *Just not yet.*

———————

Forty-five minutes later Jennie still hadn't told Gram about the letter. Of course, Gram had been sleeping most of that time. Jennie gazed down on the Irish countryside, with its green rolling hills. Stone fences separated the fields, making it look like a patchwork quilt. "It's beautiful."

"It is, isn't it." Gram leaned across Jennie as the pilot banked for his final approach into Shannon Airport. "Have you ever seen so many shades of green?" Gram's eyes filled with tears. She leaned back and wiped them away with her fingers. Something was definitely wrong.

Had Gram been threatened earlier? Probably not. Gram wasn't the sort to cry over a threat—she'd do something about it. Early on, when Gram had first invited Jennie, she had said she had some business to take care of. *But what kind of business?*

Something dangerous? Something to do with the threat? No. If Gram had been threatened before, she wouldn't have let Jennie go with her. Gram and Jennie's parents would have cancelled the reunion—and Jennie's birthday party.

Jennie chewed on her lower lip, trying to decide what to do. She couldn't explain why she hadn't mentioned the note to Gram. Well, she could, really. She didn't want to worry her—and she didn't want to go back home. Still, she needed to tell Gram in case the threat was real. So far there had been no attempt on their lives. But then, they hadn't landed yet. Jennie figured they'd be safe enough in the airport. At least until they left the secured area. Of course, Jennie planned to tell Gram long before that. Before they left the plane, she decided.

Gram wiped her palms on her black cotton slacks.

Several times since leaving Portland, Jennie had thought about asking Gram what was wrong but never did. The time never seemed right. They'd spent Monday afternoon and evening and most of Tuesday in Manhattan, shopping, eating, and sight-seeing. Their plane left Tuesday evening, and they had been flying all night. It was now Wednesday morning.

"You look worried," Jennie said, hoping maybe now Gram would talk about whatever was bothering her.

Gram leaned back, shifting her gaze from the view to Jennie. With a wry smile she said, "Am I that obvious?"

"I thought you were excited about our trip."

"I am. But I'm anxious about it too."

"Why? Is it the writing assignments?"

"Not at all. I enjoy interviewing and gathering information and photos for the articles."

"Then what?" *Are you working undercover?* Jennie decided it was too soon to ask such a probing question.

"Family. I know it sounds silly, but . . ."

"You're nervous about seeing the family?" *Could one of them have sent the mysterious note?* "Why?"

"I'm sure that seems odd to you. It'll be wonderful to see Aunt Catherine and the others. . . ." Gram clasped her hands around her knee. "It's been too long."

"Too long? What do you mean?"

"Going home." Tears gathered in Gram's eyes again.

"Oh." Jennie leaned over to touch her arm. She finally understood—or thought she did. "Because of Great-grandma Mary." Mary O'Donnell, Gram's mother, had died three years earlier, and Gram was still grieving.

"That among other things. I should have come home and stayed with her those last days. No one should have to die alone."

"Wasn't Aunt Catherine there?"

"Yes, but I was her only child."

"But you were busy with—"

"My life," Gram finished. "I didn't want to believe she was that ill. I should have been there for her."

"You didn't know," Jennie offered, though she doubted her reassurances would help.

"True. It isn't my fault that my mother died. I couldn't have stopped that, but I could have been there for her. Instead, I was playing spy games and falling in love."

"But J.B. and the government needed you." Jennie felt awkward consoling Gram. After all, what did a nearly seventeen-year-old know about such things? Jennie didn't know too many specifics, just that Gram had made a lot of trips to places like Mexico, South America, and Canada. She'd helped bring many criminals to justice. Jennie thought about the threatening note again. Was someone out to even the score?

"J.B. could have found another agent," Gram went on. "He'd been a bachelor for nearly sixty years. I'd been a widow for eleven. It wouldn't have hurt either of us to wait a few more months to fall in love." She adjusted her legs, stretching as much as possible within the confines of their seats.

The flight attendant announced that they would be landing soon and that passengers should stash their carry-ons and put their seats in an upright position.

"Well, it's too late to worry over what I should have done," Gram said philosophically. "Unfortunately, my guilt has caused me to put off the job I should have done ages ago."

"What job is that?" Jennie tucked the notes she'd made

for her family tree project into her bag and stuffed the bag under the seat.

"Taking care of my mother's estate. And facing the family."

"Facing?" Jennie grinned. "Now it sounds as though you're afraid of them."

"No." Gram smiled too. "Not in the way you think." She frowned then. "It's hard to explain. I neglected my duties as a daughter. Aunt Catherine isn't happy with me. It's been three years since my mother died, and I've only popped in for a couple of very brief visits since then."

"What do you have to do?"

"I don't know exactly. I have a bad feeling about it. No idea why."

Tell her. Jennie cleared her throat. She tried, but the words stuck there.

"Sometimes you put things off and put things off and pretty soon a year has gone by, then two—three."

Jennie could identify with that. She'd put off telling Gram about the note, and now it seemed a monumental task.

Gram leaned back in the seat, closing her eyes. "Mother left me the house and everything she owned."

"An inheritance? That doesn't sound so bad."

Giving Jennie a sideways glance, Gram said, "Would you like to help me sort through it?"

"Sure." Jennie, being naturally curious about almost everything, decided it would be a great way to spend her days while her cousins were in school. "Maybe there are some things I can use in my genealogy report."

"I'm sure there will be. I think there's an old Bible and some pictures."

"Is the house close to where we'll be staying?"

"It *is* where we'll be staying. The house is mine, but Catherine is living there with her grandson, Thomas, and his family."

"The Keegans—Thomas and Bridget." Jennie thought

back to the family tree she'd written out just a few hours earlier. "Sean and Shelagh's parents, right?" She also remembered that Catherine's son and daughter-in-law had been killed in a car accident when Thomas was ten, and Catherine had raised him.

"Right. I told them to use anything they wanted. Auntie says there is still an attic full of chests and boxes for me to go through. I'll pick out what I want of it. You can do the same. There should be some linens we can give Kate and your mother."

"Sounds like fun. I can get pictures to go with the names on my family tree."

"You might even find some skeletons locked away in our family closet," Gram added on a teasing note.

"Really?" Jennie loved the idea.

"Oh yes. Ireland has a rich history."

"A bloody one too," Jennie added. Before the trip, she'd spent some time reading about Irish history and the different invasions by the Celts and Vikings. She'd also read about the famous potato famine in the 1800s that caused Ireland's population to decrease by two million.

"Have you ever done a family history, Gram?"

"No. I've thought about it a time or two, but never did."

"Who knows? Maybe we'll discover that we're descendants of royalty or something."

"More likely we're related to some marauding Viking."

Jennie chuckled. Gram was probably right. Gram, Jennie's father, and Jennie herself all had an adventurous nature. They had chosen to go into law enforcement, and Jennie planned to follow in their footsteps. It would be fun digging up the past. But that would have to wait. They had a long drive from the airport to where they would be staying on the coast.

If you make it out of the airport. Jennie's stomach lurched at the thought.

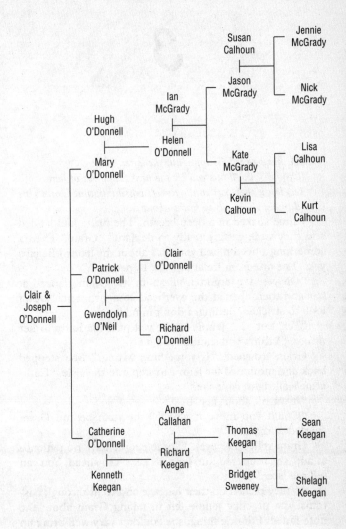

3

You have to tell Gram about the letter. Now!

If you do, she'll put you on the next plane out of here.

Yes, but if there's even the remote possibility that Gram's life is in danger, she needs to know about it.

Jennie sucked in a deep breath. The plane had landed and they were getting ready to deplane. "Gram? There's something I need to tell you—it's about the letter J.B. gave you. The one from Ireland. I . . . I opened it."

"Oh yes, I'd forgotten all about it." Gram glanced at her and then opened the overhead compartment. "Don't look so stricken, darling. I don't mind."

"Yes, but . . ." Jennie swallowed past the lump in her throat. "I think you should read it."

Gram frowned. "Is something wrong?" She stepped back and motioned for Jennie to step into the aisle. "Catherine's all right, isn't she?"

"It wasn't about her. I—"

"Could you move it along?" the man behind Gram snarled at them.

Gram rolled her eyes. "Some people have no patience at all," she muttered into Jennie's ear. "Go ahead. You can tell me later."

As they picked up their luggage and went through customs, the urgency Jennie felt in telling Gram about the note faded. For one thing, she couldn't very well bring up the subject of a threat in front of the authorities, or they'd never be allowed to leave the airport. As it was, Jennie wondered if they'd end up arresting her. The guards insisted on searching every piece of luggage Jennie had brought. Probably because she was a teenager.

When they finally escaped the customs officials, Jennie and Gram began looking for Catherine or one of the other family members. Jennie searched the crowd for a familiar face—familiar only because she'd looked over some of Gram's old photos. Gram would know them, of course, but she didn't seem to be having any luck either.

"Maybe they're late," Jennie ventured. "You said they had a ways to come. And it's only eight."

"Yes, all the way from the coast. But they're all early risers, and if I know Aunt Catherine, she'd have been here an hour ago." Gram frowned. "I hope nothing has happened."

Jennie hoped so too.

"The letter . . ." Gram reached into her bag.

"It wasn't from the family. It was just a threat."

The words hung between them, and the world around them seemed to stand still.

"A *what*?" Gram set her bags on a chair and fished the note out of her carryon.

Jennie winced. She hadn't meant it to come out that way. "A threat. I tried to tell you earlier on the plane—but then we were in customs and . . ."

Gram opened the note, and her expression—one of disbelief—turned to anger. "Who in the world. . . ?" She turned over the envelope and studied the postmark. "Mailed from Limerick."

"Looks like someone doesn't want us here. I thought maybe you were working on a case or something. I . . . I should have told you right away, but I was afraid you'd . . . You're not sending me back home, are you?"

Gram frowned and tucked the note away. "I don't know. I probably should." She glanced around. "I'm not working on an investigation."

21

"Please don't make me go home."

Gram rubbed at the creases on her brow. "We'll see. Right now we need to find Catherine or whoever is picking us up."

The crowd had dispersed, and Jennie noticed a tall, wiry man with glasses leaning against the wall and holding a placard that read *Bradley*. Jennie nudged Gram and pointed. "Does he look familiar?"

"He does, but I have no idea who he is." Gram waved at him.

"What if he's the one who sent the note?"

Before Gram could respond, the man moved away from the wall and put the card to his side, dodging a couple hurrying by. "Mrs. Bradley?" A smile spread across his handsome features. He had a regal look about him and reminded Jennie of England's Prince Charles. He was about her father's age and had a similar build.

"Yes." Gram looked him over. "I'm afraid you have me at a disadvantage. Should I know you?"

"Probably not. We met when I was younger. I'm William Kavanagh's son, Declan." His Irish accent seemed off somehow—maybe with some English and American mixed in.

"Of course." Gram brightened. "I see the resemblance. No wonder you looked familiar. But I thought you were living in the U.S."

"I was. Moved back to Ireland a couple years ago with my software company." Declan's gaze moved from Gram to Jennie. "And you must be Jennie. I've heard a great deal about you."

"You have?" She wasn't sure she liked the idea of his knowing too much. Could he be trusted? What if he'd sent the threat?

"It's all good, I can assure you. My father likes to keep tabs on your family."

Before Jennie could ask why, Gram interrupted with an introduction. "Jennie, this is Declan Kavanagh, a family friend." Gram's gaze traveled over the few people left outside of customs. "Did you come alone?"

"Yes. I hope you're not too disappointed. When I heard you were coming, I offered to pick you up. No sense in the Keegans making a trip when I'm already here."

"No, of course not. We'll see them soon enough." Gram adjusted the strap of her bag. She seemed relieved.

Jennie was disappointed but didn't say so. She'd worked herself up to meeting her relatives. Now she'd have to be nervous all over again. Nor did she like the idea of going off with a stranger. Well, not a stranger, exactly, but he could have written the note. He could be planning to take them out in the country to kill them.

Don't go there, McGrady. Jennie looked from Declan to Gram. She seemed completely at ease with him. *You worry too much. You told Gram about the threat. Let her deal with it. If she trusts Declan, you can too.* Jennie relaxed some. He seemed friendly enough. Still, she planned to keep an eye on him.

"Well, then, let's be going." Declan began walking through the terminal. "We've a bit of a drive."

Jennie set her backpack on top of her luggage and pulled them along behind her, thankful for the wheels. So far they seemed safe enough. There were guards posted at intervals, so Jennie wasn't too worried yet.

"They're well, aren't they?" Gram asked. "The Keegans, I mean."

"Except for Catherine. She's had an accident, you know. Broke her leg."

"Catherine. . . ?" Gram stopped.

"You didn't know?" Declan put an arm around Gram's shoulders.

"I had no idea," Gram said. "When?"

"Last week. I thought they'd told you."

Gram shook her head and began walking again. "What happened?"

"She was riding her bicycle and rounded a bend just as

a tourist came through. Hit her head on. Luckily the driver wasn't speeding. Still, Catherine flew over the handlebars and landed in the hedgerows."

"How badly was she hurt?"

"Badly enough. Though to hear her tell it, it was just a scratch."

"A broken leg doesn't sound like a scratch to me." Gram sighed. "Not at her age."

"Better not let her hear you say that."

"Hmm," Gram mused. "Still hasn't slowed down?"

"She just got out of the hospital on Monday. Insisted she be home when you got there."

Gram shook her head. "They should have called."

"You know how stubborn Catherine is. She probably didn't want to worry you."

Gram agreed. "How like her."

Jennie hurried to keep up with them. She wished she could have thought of something comforting or reassuring to say to Gram, but nothing came to mind. Poor Gram, losing her mother, and now Aunt Catherine being hurt. And the threat. It didn't seem fair.

When they reached the exit, Gram excused herself, saying she needed to call J.B. before leaving the airport. When she came back, she told Declan about the threat.

"Any idea who sent it?" he asked.

"None. To my knowledge I haven't made any enemies in Ireland. Can't think of a soul who might not want me here."

Declan shook his head. "Nor can I."

"I hope you don't mind," Gram said, "but I really should talk to the Limerick police."

"Not at all. It's on our way. Perhaps they can figure it out."

"Let's hope so. They may be able to lift prints from the note—or trace it."

They left the airport and piled into Declan's Mercedes convertible, Gram in the front and Jennie in the back. The steering wheel was on the opposite side of the car. Though Jennie knew the Irish drove on the left side of the road, she wondered if she'd ever get used to it. For the entire twenty-four kilometers into Limerick, Jennie sat white-knuckled, expecting a crash at any minute.

They dropped Gram off in front of the police station, and then Jennie and Declan went to find a place to park.

Jennie was more than miffed that Gram insisted on talking to the police alone. Declan took Jennie to a nearby pastry and gift shop across from the police station to wait. They talked a little about the plane trip, and then Declan's cell phone rang. While Jennie waited for him, she had tea and a cream cheese and berry pastry. Declan was still talking when she finished, so she wandered around looking at the gift items.

After only twenty minutes, Gram emerged from the police station. Jennie stepped out of the shop and waved at her. Gram waved back and began to cross the street. As Gram stepped off the curb, a van careened around the corner and headed straight for her.

Jennie screamed. Tires screeched. When Jennie opened her eyes, her grandmother had disappeared.

4

Declan raced across the street.

Jennie's legs finally unfroze enough to follow him. Several uniformed officers emerged from the station. Jennie elbowed her way into the circle. "Gram! Are you okay?"

Gram was on her knees. "A little shaken up, but I'll live." She took the hand Declan offered and got to her feet.

"Did you get a look at the driver?" Declan asked.

Gram shook her head. "Happened too fast."

One of the officers had taken off running in the direction the van had gone. Another took a car. Still another took hold of Gram's other arm. "I'm terrible sorry, ma'am," he said. "Can we call an ambulance for ye?"

"No. I'm fine. Just skinned my knee."

The officers began questioning the people who had gathered around, asking for information about the hit-and-run vehicle. No one seemed to be able to offer much more than that the van had been white—probably a utility van. There had been no distinguishing features, and no one had gotten a license number. Nor could anyone identify the driver.

Gram filled out an incident report and finished answering questions. Within a half hour they were out on the street again.

As they left the station, Gram wrapped her arms around Jennie. "Don't look so worried, darling. I'm all right, really. The only real concern I have is for you."

"They aren't after me, Gram. They're after you."

"True. But just the same, I feel as though I should send you home."

"No, please don't."

Declan pulled his car up to the curb.

"We'll talk about it later," Gram said as they climbed in. Jennie folded her arms and pouted in the backseat while Gram used Declan's cell phone to call the airport to find a flight out.

After a few minutes she set the phone aside. "There's nothing available for the next three days."

"Good. There's no reason to send me back anyway. Like I said, they aren't after me."

Gram just looked at Jennie, her gaze full of concern.

"You should be safe enough. The inspector assured us that his people would find the van."

"Let's hope so."

Jennie scrunched down in the seat and fussed at herself for not being more observant. *You should have gone with Gram*, she told herself. *You might have seen it coming. You might have gotten a license number or been able to identify the driver.*

And you might have gotten yourself killed.

Gram had told her not to worry, but Jennie couldn't help it. Every few minutes she scanned the traffic for the white van.

As the traffic lessened and they reached the countryside, Jennie's fears subsided. There had been no sign of the van. She relaxed some. But not much. How could she, with a death threat hanging over their heads?

A cool wind whipped at her hair, pulling loose the shorter strands from the French braid she'd painstakingly woven just before landing. Oh well. So much for wanting to impress the relatives. "Get real, McGrady," she muttered to herself. "Do you really think they care about your hair?" Mom would have told her, "Just be yourself. They'll love you."

"Right." Ordering herself to stop worrying and enjoy the view, Jennie leaned back in the seat. She relished the sense of freedom she felt being on the ground again. Normally, Jennie didn't mind flying, but going over the ocean had been a little scary.

"Did you hear that, Jennie?" Gram shouted so Jennie could hear her above the road noise.

Jennie shook her head. She hadn't heard anything other than the car engine and wind. She leaned forward. "What?"

"Declan has offered to let us stay at the castle. What do you think?"

Her dark thoughts scattered. "A castle? Really?"

"Really." Gram laughed. "Declan says we might be safer there. It might be best since Bridget has her hands full with Aunt Catherine right now. Their place isn't all that big—four bedrooms and an attic. I imagine the family pretty well fills it up."

Jennie's grin widened. "I'd love it."

"Somehow I thought you might."

"What about Aunt Catherine? Will she be upset?"

"We'll visit her often. I doubt she'll mind too much."

"I thought you'd be more comfortable in the castle." Declan glanced back at Jennie through the rearview mirror.

"That's very kind of you," Gram said. "You're sure William won't mind?"

"Who's William?" Jennie asked.

"My father."

"Oh, right." Jennie vaguely remembered Declan saying something about William when he'd introduced himself.

"He's thrilled about it."

"William and I were friends growing up," Gram explained to Jennie. Turning back to Declan, she asked, "How is he, anyway?"

"Dad's doing well. Retired now, but he manages to

keep busy. Spends a lot of time on the golf course and with the horses."

"Horses?" Jennie perked up. "You have horses?"

"Forty or so. Do you like to ride?"

"Love it." Threat or no, this was getting better all the time.

"Good. Jeremy—that's my son—and your cousins go out at least twice a week. I'm certain they've an outing planned for you."

"Great."

Jennie leaned back again, letting the wind carry away the discussion Declan and Gram were having. She could hardly take it all in. A castle. Horses. If she'd been standing she'd have jumped in the air and cheered. Now all she could do was grin. *Gram and I will be staying in a castle.* Gram had mentioned visiting some of the many authentic and ancient castles during their trip. That was one of the things Gram had said she wanted to include in her articles. But to actually stay in one . . . More than ever Jennie wished Lisa were there to share this time with her. *She'll be so jealous when I tell her.* Jennie felt an even wider grin ease across her face. She probably looked ridiculous but didn't care.

Declan's laugh brought Jennie back to their conversation. "Of course it's haunted," he said, apparently answering Gram's question. "No self-respecting castle in Ireland would be without a few ghosts."

Jennie gulped back a response. "Haunted?"

5

Gram glanced back at Jennie and with a mischievous grin said, "Don't worry, darling. Most of the ghosts I've met are relatively harmless."

"Oh, that's reassuring." Jennie grinned. Despite the thought of sharing their living quarters with *ghosts*, which she didn't really believe in, she still looked forward to staying at the castle. Still, the idea was a bit scary.

Shaking thoughts of ghosts from her mind, Jennie turned her attention to the Irish countryside. They'd left the busy and noisy city of Limerick behind and were heading west. Gram had showed her their destination on the map. The small village of Callaway was situated on the south side of Kerry Head. Before long, exhaustion from the long trip and the purr of the car's engine lulled Jennie to sleep.

"Jennie," Gram said softly.

Jennie started. "Are we there?" The road had become even narrower. Stone fences lined both sides. Jennie hoped they didn't have to pass another car—she doubted there'd be room. She heard bleating and straightened to see several long-haired sheep moseying down the middle of the road. The creamy white bodies were accentuated by their black faces and hooves.

Declan honked the horn, but the sheep stayed in the road. He eased his way along, and finally the sheep moved aside, giving them just enough room to pass. A few minutes later they stopped near a huge gray building with a steep green roof and high steeples.

"Is this the castle?" Jennie asked.

Declan chuckled. "No. The castle is yonder. You can see it on the rise. Just beyond it is the Atlantic Ocean."

Jennie squinted to see better. The castle, with its turrets and multilevel design, looked enormous even in the distance. Excitement tingled through her at the thought of exploring it. "What's this, then?" She turned back around to look at the building they'd parked beside. "Looks like a church."

"That's because it is," Gram offered. "This is Saint Matthew's, the church my mother and I attended when I lived here. My parents are both buried here, along with my grandparents." Gram pointed to a stone fence to the left of the building. Behind it, Jennie could see a cemetery. "I asked Declan to stop. I wanted to visit the graves. Thought you might want to see where your ancestors are buried."

Jennie almost said, "What for?" but thought better of it. Visiting graves was something adults did. She didn't especially like the idea, but her mother had told her visiting the graves of family members and friends and bringing flowers on special days was a way of paying respect and honoring their lives.

Jennie followed Declan and Gram to the open gate and inside the cemetery. She'd been in only one cemetery. It didn't look anything like this. The one she'd visited—where her grandpa Calhoun had been buried—had mostly flat marble headstones. There'd been some old markers and a few statues, but not this many. Here, many of the tombs were above the ground, made of stone or marble; some had statues, others ornate crosses. One of the headstones bore the date 1482. Some were probably even older.

The grounds were beautifully kept. Jennie's gaze swept over the large area and rested on the probable cause. A large man in coveralls, most likely the gardener, maneuvered a wheelbarrow around a tight corner and paused to pull some weeds before disappearing behind a large tomb.

A door on the side of the church opened, and a man in a clerical collar and a black shirt and pants stepped out.

"Can I help you?" he asked in a heavy Irish accent. He was an older man of average build, maybe in his seventies. He was balding, and wisps of white hair ruffled in the wind as he came toward them. He frowned slightly as his gaze lingered on Declan. "Declan Kavanagh, isn't it?" Though the two men shook hands, Jennie sensed an animosity between them.

"Yes. I brought a visitor."

"Hello, Father." Gram held out her hand. "Helen Bradley . . . um, Mary O'Donnell's daughter."

The priest's face lit up, and he gave Gram's hand a vigorous shake. "Helen O'Donnell. Of course. And aren't I sorry I didn't recognize you right off. How long has it been now, three years?"

"Yes. I've been meaning to get back, but . . ."

"Well, now. You're here. Isn't that what matters?" His blue eyes twinkled as he turned to Jennie. "And who might this be?"

"My granddaughter Jennie McGrady. Jason's oldest. Jennie, this is Father O'Roarke."

"Aye, and isn't she the spitting image of you." He shook Jennie's hand. "Welcome to Ireland, Jennie, and especially to Saint Matthew's. I hope you'll be joining us for Sunday Mass."

Jennie glanced at Gram, not sure what to say.

"We'll be here, Father," Gram answered. "You can be sure of that."

"Have ye seen Catherine, then?" the priest asked.

"Not yet. Declan just picked us up at the airport, but I wanted to stop and see the graves."

"Ah, and rightly ye should. Come, I'll take you to them."

Father O'Roarke meandered around the stones and

tombs, coming to a stop at the opposite wall. There were six graves marked with the O'Donnell name. Jennie's great-grandparents Hugh and Mary O'Donnell were buried side by side beneath blocks of marble engraved with their names and the dates of their births and deaths. Atop Mary's marble stone was a tall, ornately carved Celtic cross. The two raised tombstones were connected by a large slab of stone. Similar stones identified the burial places of Clair and Joseph O'Donnell, Mary's parents, and Margaret and Jack O'Donnell, Hugh's parents.

While working on her family tree, Jennie had thought it strange that both Mary and Hugh would have the same last name. She'd asked Gram about it on the plane trip, and Gram had explained that Hugh and Mary had been distant cousins.

Gram showed Jennie three other graves—one of Catherine's husband, Kenneth Keegan, and their son and daughter-in-law, Richard and Anne, who'd been killed in a car accident. Fresh flowers had been laid in front of each headstone.

"Catherine sent Shelagh with flowers just this morning," Father O'Roarke explained. "Usually comes in once a week, she does."

Gram ran her hand over the cross and stone and traced the letters in Mary's name.

"I'll leave you to your thoughts," the priest said softly, touching Gram's shoulder. "If you need me, I'll be inside."

Gram nodded. "Thank you."

"I'll be in the car." Declan turned to go as well. He and Father O'Roarke talked briefly as they walked away, but Jennie couldn't hear their conversation. Though he seemed pleasant enough, she had the feeling Declan felt uncomfortable about being there.

For that matter, so do you.

Turning her attention back to Gram, Jennie watched her grandmother kneel as she made the sign of the cross. Puzzled, Jennie looked away, her gaze moving to the stone wall and the hills beyond. Gram's actions and the church and Father O'Roarke filled Jennie with questions. She'd always thought of Gram as being a Protestant like herself, but this church and Father O'Roarke were definitely Catholic. Jennie was seeing a side of Gram she'd never seen before. She put her questions aside for later and focused again on Mary's grave, trying to imagine what she'd been like.

Jennie had seen her great-grandmother Mary only once, and that had been years ago when Jennie was five. She and her parents and Gram had come to Ireland for a visit. Though she'd seen photos, Jennie didn't remember anything about it. That saddened her. This was a part of the family she knew about but didn't really know. Now it was too late—for Mary, at least.

When Jennie turned her attention back to Gram, she was kneeling beside her father's grave. Unlike Mary's ornate cross, Hugh O'Donnell's had a simple headstone. He'd died in 1945, when Gram was a little girl.

Jennie blinked back tears as sorrow for Gram washed over her. It was hard to imagine what things must have been like for her growing up. Gram had never talked much about her childhood. Most of what Jennie knew about Ireland she'd learned from her own studies. But Gram had told Jennie that they'd been poor. But also very fortunate, as Mary's brother, Patrick, or Uncle Paddy, had provided for them. He'd recently died and left Gram a lot of money and part ownership of a castle resort in the San Juan Islands.

Gram rose and settled an arm around Jennie's shoulders. "We'd best be going, sweetheart. Declan's waiting."

"I didn't know you were Catholic," Jennie said as they walked.

"Really?" Gram seemed surprised. "I suppose it never came up."

Jennie looked up at her for more information, but none came. "But you've always gone to a Protestant church."

Gram smiled and hugged Jennie to her. "I was raised Catholic."

Jennie had read about the history of Ireland and how Saint Patrick had established the Catholic Church and how later Cromwell had fought to bring in the Church of England. She'd also studied about the terrible bombings in Northern Ireland. "Is there a lot of fighting in this part of Ireland between the Catholics and Protestants?"

"Mmm. Used to be. I understand many of their differences have been resolved. But I suspect the antagonism is still there."

Antagonism. Was that what Jennie had seen in Declan's face when he left the graveyard to wait in his car? "Is Declan Protestant?"

"Yes." Again no explanation.

"Why did you convert?"

"From Catholicism to Protestantism?" Gram sighed. "I never did, really. Your grandfather, Ian, was an Anglican." Her lips formed a thin smile. "My mother was terribly upset about that. He managed to convince her that he would never force me to change my beliefs."

"But you did."

"Not really. I'm a Christian. Always have been. My faith in God is stronger and more stable than before, but not all that different. We worship the same God. Our basic beliefs are the same."

The conversation ended as they piled back into the car. Soon they were heading toward the castle. Declan talked as they went, pointing out this neighbor and that. A short distance later they passed through the small coastal village of Callaway. The main street was lined with small shops and a place called Mulhaney's Pub. In a clothing store window, Jennie saw an Aran sweater in a misty gray lavender she'd like to have. It reminded her of heather.

On the water was a marina with a wide variety of boats. A large fishing boat was heading out toward the open sea.

They drove west through town and turned south,

going past the marina, and were soon going down another narrow lane. About a mile out of town they came to a two-story white farmhouse with a barn and several outbuildings. Cattle and sheep grazed in the surrounding pastureland.

Declan slowed but didn't pull into the driveway. "Do you want to stop now or go to the castle to freshen up first?"

Gram glanced at the house hesitantly and then looked at her watch.

"We've invited the entire family for dinner at the castle this evening," Declan went on. "If you'd rather wait, that's all right too."

Jennie looked at her watch as well. It was after ten.

"Let's stop, but just for a minute. I'm anxious for Jennie to meet Catherine and see the house I grew up in."

Jennie took a deep breath. She was nervous about meeting the family, but even more, she was worried that one of them might have sent the threatening note and tried to run Gram down. Maybe the Keegans were worried about Gram's being there. After all, Gram owned the farm. They stood to lose a great deal if Gram decided to sell it out from under them. Jennie directed her gaze over the house and land. Everything seemed peaceful enough. There were several vehicles in the yard—a tractor, a battered pickup, but no white van. At least not yet.

6

They're family, McGrady. Not killers. Jennie reined in her imagination. *These people love Gram.* Still, it might be interesting to see samples of their handwriting.

"The farm was once part of the Kavanagh estate," Gram told Jennie. "My father and mother moved in when Dad worked for the Kavanaghs as a grounds keeper. He eventually bought it. And I inherited it when my mother died."

"Are you going to keep it?" Jennie asked, still wondering about a motive.

"For now, I suppose—the Keegans have done me a huge favor caring for it."

"What would happen to them if you sold it?" Jennie couldn't help asking.

"They'd have to find something else, I suppose." Gram smiled. "But I don't think we need to worry about that right now."

Jennie's gaze roamed across the green pasture to the east, where velvety fields were interrupted by stone fences. Some of the fences still stood, others had been scattered. To the west the ocean pounded at cliffs not more than a football field's length away. She'd seen pictures of the house when Gram had lived there. Though she couldn't see it from the house, there would be a path down to the water and a dock.

Jennie vividly remembered one picture of Gram as a

young girl of about twelve and a boy about the same age holding up a string of fish between them. Gram had mentioned more than once that though the family was poor, the sea always provided enough food. Their ancestors had not been so severely affected by the big potato famine as many of the others who lived inland.

As if reading Jennie's thoughts, Gram said, "I loved living here, near the shore. I suppose that's why I love the Oregon beach so much. Willie—Declan's father—and I used to go fishing nearly every day. We'd sell our fish at the market in town." She cast Jennie a wistful smile. "He kept very little of the money for himself. At the end of the day there would always be twice as much money as I thought there should be. For years I thought I was just poor at math. Later I realized William had been pocketing a few cents for spending money and giving me the rest." She reached up to brush away the tears her sentiments had brought. "Your father was a generous man, Declan."

"True enough," Declan agreed. "He still is. Sometimes to a fault." He glanced at Gram and shrugged. "But I suppose it is better to be too generous than to be the least bit greedy."

Declan turned into the gravel driveway, and as he did, a large black Labrador, nearly as tall as the car, bounded around from the side of the house and yipped at the car. Declan drove slowly, watching the dog prancing alongside them. "Settle down, Gracie. It's just me. Behave yourself, now."

A young girl with red hair popped open the door and raced across the porch, down the steps, and into the yard. Jennie's breath caught. She looked so much like Lisa, Jennie had to remind herself that Lisa was half a world away.

"There's a good dog, Gracie. Come along," the girl said.

The dog ran to his mistress and licked at her hand as she tried to pet her.

"That's Shelagh," Gram told Jennie.

Declan chuckled. "She's been beside herself waiting for you to show up. Apparently her enthusiasm's rubbed off on the dog."

"Mum! Grandie! Da!" Shelagh rushed to the car, nearly colliding with it. "Come quick. They're here."

The girl's wide grin revealed a shiny set of braces. Her face was flushed and, unlike Lisa, she had no freckles. She wasn't as beautiful as Lisa, but cute with a round face, a darling smile, and dimples.

Gram opened her door, and Shelagh extended her hand and pumped it up and down. Gracie crowded in, sniffing at Gram and not moving until Gram petted her.

"Welcome to Ireland, Cousin Helen. We're more than a bit glad you've come. Sean and I missed school today so we could be here when you arrived."

Jennie eased her slender frame out of the backseat while Shelagh jumped up and down. The girl grabbed Jennie's hand. "You must be Jennie. 'Tis pleased I am to meet my American cousin."

Gracie moved from Gram to Jennie, wagging her tail and licking Jennie's hand. Jennie laughed at their enthusiasm as she bent down to stroke the dog's silky black coat. "Hi, Gracie."

When Jennie straightened, Shelagh took Jennie's hand and dragged her toward the house and the open door. "Come and meet my brother, Sean. He's your age. I'm fourteen. Sean said you wouldn't be wantin' to hang around with a runt like me, but you will, won't you, Jennie?" Her eyes grew rounder. She seemed genuinely concerned that her brother might be right.

"That's silly." Jennie didn't quite know what to say. "You don't look like a runt to me."

A woman near Jennie's own mother's age came out the door next. She wiped her hands on a white apron. Jennie could see immediately where Shelagh got her roundness and red hair. Behind her came a boy Jennie thought must be Shelagh's brother. She saw why he might call his sister a runt. Sean stood about six feet tall and seemed a bit too thin for his height. He had deep chestnut hair and a face full of freckles. He stopped on the bottom step of the porch, his cool gaze drifting over Jennie.

Jennie's first instinct had been to turn away, but she didn't. If he wanted to be rude, she could be rude back. She met his stare and returned one of her own. While Jennie and Sean sized each other up, Gram and Bridget hugged like long-lost friends.

"Now, aren't we glad you stopped to see us before heading to the castle. Herself has been asking after you all morning."

With their thick Irish accents, Jennie was having a hard time understanding them. They had an odd way of using pronouns and phrasing statements as questions. Herself, in this case, must have been Aunt Catherine. Gram didn't seem to be having any trouble understanding them at all.

"I was anxious to see all of you as well." Gram looped an arm around Jennie's shoulders and drew her forward. "You remember Jennie."

"Of course." Bridget took Jennie into her arms. Jennie had to lean down to hug her. She smelled of spice cake and apple pie. Jennie felt nearly as comfortable in her embrace as she did with her own mother. Bridget stood back, assessing her and holding Jennie's hands in both of hers. "Sure and haven't you grown, Jennie. Pictures just don't do the job, now, do they? And haven't ye turned into a lovely young woman."

Sean *harumphed*, apparently not agreeing.

"Sean Keegan," his mother said sharply. "Where are your manners? Come give your cousins a warm welcome."

Sean, looking as uncomfortable as a cowboy in a tuxedo, jumped off the step and with his hands stuffed into his pockets said hello. A slight grin curved the corners of his mouth. He was shy, Jennie realized, not mean. Jennie started to tell him she wasn't the least bit dangerous, when Gram pulled him into a hug and told him what a handsome young man he'd become.

His face turned ten shades of red.

"Well, now, let's not be standing out here all day," Bridget crooned. "I've tea and scones on the table. We'd best be getting you inside to see Grandie."

"How is Catherine?" Gram asked. "Declan told us she'd broken a leg."

"True enough," Bridget answered. "The doctors say she has a good chance of a full recovery, but at her age, it's hard to know." Then she clucked, "Except for the crutches and the cast, you'd never know she'd been hurt."

"Crutches? At her age?"

"Ach now, you don't want to hear about that one. Old Dr. Walsh insisted she use a wheelchair. Grandie would have no part in it. Made us buy her a pair of crutches, she did." Bridget sighed. "Seems to be getting on just fine with them."

Gram nodded. "I wish you'd called when it happened."

"I suppose I should have," Bridget agreed in an apologetic tone. "I started to write, but I didn't think the letter would reach you before you left."

"It's all right. I feel badly, though. I'd have come to help care for her."

"It's been no trouble, really. The children and Thomas are a big help. Sean worries over her like a mother hen."

That surprised Jennie. She hadn't taken Sean for being the sensitive type.

Bridget put a hand to each of their backs and turned toward Declan.

"Will you be coming in, then, Declan?" Bridget asked.

"Sounds tempting, but if it's all the same, I'll wait out here. Is Thomas about?"

"You'll find him in the barn, I think. Sean, run tell your father we've company."

Sean caught and held Jennie's gaze in another strange challenge she couldn't read. She had the feeling he didn't like her but had no idea why.

Shelagh seemed to have caught the interchange. As they followed Gram and Bridget up the steps onto a large wraparound porch, Shelagh stopped Jennie and whispered, "Don't mind him. He's suspicious of everyone he doesn't know. Especially rich Yanks. And even more if they're Prots."

"Prots?" Jennie grimaced. "What's that? Sounds like some kind of sausage."

Shelagh howled with laughter. Once she caught her breath she gasped, "I'm sorry, Jennie. I'm not meaning to laugh at you, but—" She burst into another fit of laughter. Finally gaining control of herself, Shelagh offered, "Protestants." She continued up the porch steps and hurriedly explained, "Sure and I don't mind a bit that you and Cousin Helen are Prots. We don't around here—not anymore—well, most don't. The Kavanaghs are Prots, don't you know. But we like them just the same. There's a fair bit of trouble over it up north. Mum says we believe in the same God and all. Only trouble we'll be having—well, not me, actually, but Grandie—is seeing Helen give up her Catholic ways to become one of them. Anyway, it's not so much the faith issue. It's more political than that. Has to do with the way the Brits came in and took us over. But that was a long time ago. Not something for us to concern ourselves about now."

Before Jennie had a chance to respond, Shelagh pulled her across the porch. "You'll be wanting to come up to my room, Jennie. I want to show you my CD collection."

"You'll do no such thing, Shelagh Keegan. Jennie will want to meet Catherine. And soon after that they'll be off to the castle. You'll have plenty of time to show her your room tomorrow."

Shelagh sighed. "I'm wishing you weren't staying at the castle," she muttered. "I told me mum I'd be glad to be sleeping on the floor. You could have my bed."

"That's very kind of you, Shelagh," Gram said, "but we don't want to put you out."

"Shelagh, we've talked about this already. The castle will be far more comfortable. The Kavanaghs have been more than kind to offer. It's close by, and you'll be seeing Jennie every day."

" 'Tisn't the same, Mum." Shelagh gave Jennie a look of concern. "I'd not be wanting my cousin spending her nights in that drafty old castle."

Jennie thought it best not to comment. She didn't want to hurt Shelagh's feelings, but she didn't want to offer to stay at the house either. Not when she could stay at the castle.

"Well, now. Are you coming in, or do you plan to camp out on the porch all day?"

Jennie started at the appearance of the older woman who met them at the door. She leaned heavily on a pair of crutches.

"Grandie!" Bridget hurried to Catherine's side. "What are you doing up? You were supposed to wait for one of us to fetch you."

"Humph. I'd still be in bed if I waited for you, now, wouldn't I?" The white-haired woman, looking every bit of her seventy-six years, reached one hand out toward Gram while the other clutched the wooden crutch handle.

"But the doctor said—"

"Never mind what the doctor said. Are you going to stand there yammering at me, or are we going to invite our guests in? Helen . . . it's about time you got here."

"You're as feisty as ever, I see."

Despite her obviously cantankerous nature, Catherine's eyes glistened with tears when Gram bent over to kiss her.

"Auntie, I've missed you so much." Gram turned to Jennie and motioned her over.

Jennie joined her grandmother and smiled at her great-great-aunt and leaned forward to kiss her softly wrinkled cheek. "Hello, Aunt Catherine."

"You're all grown-up." Catherine gripped her hand as

Jennie went to take a step back. "Just a bit of a thing you were when last you visited." Tears shone again in her faded blue eyes. She nodded at Gram. "Looks just like you and the twins."

"Yes, she does." Gram slipped an arm around Jennie's shoulders and hugged her close.

Jennie beamed. She loved looking like the twins, Gram's only children—Jason, Jennie's dad, and Kate, Lisa's mother. They were both tall and lanky with navy blue eyes.

They finally went inside. The house was comfortable looking and roomy. The spacious kitchen opened into a small but cozy sitting room. A braided oval rug covered the center of the hardwood floor. The kitchen and dining room had a fireplace that took up most of the wall. A functional fireplace for sure, as a huge black kettle hung in the hearth bubbling with soup or stew—most likely lunch. The aroma set Jennie's stomach to growling, and she found herself wishing for a bowl. The meaty scent of the soup mingled with that of freshly baked bread and spicy cookies. Two loaves of bread sat on a counter cooling, having come, Jennie suspected, from the oven set into the fireplace wall. The cookies lined a white linen towel in the center of the table.

Catherine heaped a plate with scones.

Bridget took the plate. "Sit yourself down, Grandie. I'll take care of the serving while you entertain our guests."

Catherine grumbled but dutifully set aside her crutches and sat down at the table.

"Would you like some tea, Jennie?" Bridget set the scones on the table and poured tea into four cups. "Shelagh, luv, come get the clotted cream and preserves."

"Yes, Mum."

Gram pulled a chair close and sat down next to Catherine.

"Where's J.B.?" Catherine asked.

"He'll be here soon. Had to finish a project at home."

Gram poured milk into her tea and began to tell Catherine about J.B. and the rest of the family. "Jason and Susan will be joining us as well," she explained. "We were hoping Kate and Kevin could come too, but I'm not sure they can get away. Kevin is still trying to work out a flight schedule."

Jennie raised an eyebrow. "I thought they weren't coming."

"Did you? I'll have to call and see if they've decided for certain." Gram turned toward the kitchen. "Can I help with anything, Bridget?"

"Not at all. Just make yourselves comfortable."

Tea and scones were one of Jennie's favorite treats. She topped her scone with clotted cream and strawberry preserves and relished every bite.

"Come on, then, Jennie," Shelagh urged when she'd finished. "I'll show you my room. It won't be as grand as anything you have in America, but . . ."

"I told you that will have to wait, Shelagh," Bridget said. "We need to be giving Helen and Jennie a chance to rest from their long trip. You'll have plenty of opportunity to show her around tomorrow."

Jennie hoped she didn't look too relieved. The trip had worn her out, and resting for a few hours sounded wonderful. Besides, she was excited to see the castle. Jennie still couldn't believe she would actually be staying there.

Shelagh sighed. "You're so lucky to be living in America. I'm going to live there myself someday."

Sean folded his arms across his chest and leaned against the doorframe. "Don't think you'll be going anytime soon. Not if Mum and Da have anything to say about it." To Jennie he said, "My sister wants to become a famous singer." The disdain in his voice left no doubt of his disapproval. "She's foolish enough to imagine she'll have enough money!"

"That's enough, Sean," his mother snapped. "There'll be no bickering between the two of you in front of our guests." Shaking her head, she glared at them with what must be the international exasperated-mother look. Jennie had seen it in her own mother's eyes often enough.

After a few lingering good-byes and a promise to see everyone again at dinner, Gram, Jennie, and Declan drove off. Minutes later, as they turned into a narrow lane that winded between long rows of cypress trees, Jennie realized that she hadn't had an opportunity to look for samples of handwriting from any of the family. She wished Gram hadn't given the note to the authorities. Jennie remembered it had been handwritten in a bold scrawl, and she made a promise to herself to examine everyone's handwriting as soon as possible.

Jennie couldn't help noticing the contrast between the beautifully manicured grounds around the castle and the haphazard look of the farm. While the Keegans' home boasted colorful spring flowers in neatly kept beds and grasses, it seemed almost unkempt compared to the castle grounds.

The closer they came to the castle, the more Jennie could see the class difference between these wealthy people and her family with their modest income. Though they dressed well enough, Jennie wondered if Sean might be right in his assessment. Maybe Shelagh's dream of coming to the U.S. would be impossible for them. *Well, not impossible. But difficult.* Jennie wondered briefly if Gram would consider buying a ticket for Shelagh and Sean to come to Portland for a visit.

"Looks like something out of Camelot," Jennie mused. "I half expect to see a knight in armor riding toward us."

Declan nodded. "I feel that way at times myself. The original castle was built in the fourteenth century."

"And it's been in your family all that time?"

"It has. We're rather proud of our heritage. In early Irish history the Kavanaghs were rulers." He smiled. "I like to think we still are."

"Does that mean we should call your father King William?" Gram chuckled.

Declan returned her laugh. "He'd probably split his sides laughing over that. A lot of the locals just call him Willie."

As they neared the magnificent structure, Jennie held her breath. "Awesome," was about all she could manage. The structure looked like what she'd seen in travel-magazine pictures or read about in Gothic novels. Made of gray stone, it stood five stories high, with turrets or towers at each corner. Between the turrets were a number of what looked like cutouts. Jennie could imagine ancient warriors shooting arrows down at their enemies. Someone was up there now looking down at them and waving.

"Who's that?" Jennie pointed.

Declan laughed. "King Willie."

Gram waved up at him. He disappeared then, apparently on his way to meet them.

Jennie caught a movement out of the corner of her eye. On the second floor in one of the turrets, someone else was watching as well. Jennie couldn't see the person, only the movement of curtains. Whoever it was stood in the shadows as if he or she didn't want to be seen. Jennie thought about asking but didn't. She rather liked the mystery of it all. She felt like a character in a Gothic mystery where the heroine comes to an enchanting castle only to find it filled with dark, sinister secrets. Were the Kavanaghs hiding something? Had one of them sent Gram the threat? Had they tried to carry it out? Was the castle really haunted?

Jennie rolled her eyes at her silly imaginings. *These people are wealthy. Gram wouldn't be a threat to them. And as for the ghosts . . . You don't believe in them, remember?* Even so, excitement pumped through Jennie's veins as Declan brought his car to a stop in front of the castle.

7

The castle was even more beautiful inside than out. The Kavanagh clan had plenty of money, no doubt about that. The entry reminded Jennie of a hotel lobby, with its marble floor and center table on which stood a vase almost as tall as she, filled with an arrangement that was probably real. The room was round, and Jennie found herself surrounded by portraits, probably of several generations of Kavanaghs.

The domed ceiling had been painted in a Michelangelo style, and Jennie was about to comment on it when an older man hurried toward them. His arms outstretched, he made a beeline for Gram. He was a tall man, well over six feet. Jennie estimated his weight to be around two hundred pounds.

"Helen . . ." He hugged Gram and then held her away from him to look her over. "You're looking more lovely every time I see you." Unlike Declan, William had a definite Irish brogue. It reminded Jennie of J.B.'s, as she detected some English accent as well.

Gram actually blushed but seemed to recover. Laughing at his compliment, she said, "Willie, you always did know how to turn a lady's head. You're looking good yourself."

"It's a pleasure to have you staying with us. When the Keegans told me you were coming, I insisted you stay here. Welcome to our humble home."

"Humble?" Gram glanced around and to the ceiling. "It's hardly that. You've made some changes since I was here last."

"Aye, that we have, luv. Thanks to my rich young son. Declan is having the entire place updated. Lord knows it needed work. Place was falling down around us."

"This looks like more than a standard remodel. The ceiling must have cost a fortune."

"Actually, it didn't cost much more than a summer's tuition at the new art institute in Dublin." Pride shone in William's eyes as his gaze moved over the cherubic scene and clouds painted on the ceiling.

"Not Sean," Gram gasped.

"The very same. He was determined to study art but couldn't afford it," William explained. "We offered to help the boy out, but Thomas, proud man that he is, wouldn't allow Sean to accept charity. So we compromised—in exchange for the tuition he needed, Sean painted this." William gestured upward. "I think we got the better end of the deal."

"I knew he had a talent for art, but this . . . It's magnificent. Is he painting commercially, then?"

"Not yet. Oh, he's done dozens of paintings, and some are in the local art galleries, but none of this caliber."

"If he's this good, why is he going to art school?" Jennie asked, trying to connect the brilliant painting to the cousin she'd just met.

William nodded. "He's good, Jennie, but not great. He has a great deal to learn about the arts and about himself. The school will mature him and give him direction."

Jennie and Gram both stared at the painting of angelic beings circling the dome. At the center was a bright light that seemed to come from heaven. The light faded, turning to blue as it touched an earthy landscape and a scattering of small figures who seemed oblivious to the heavens. Soft pastels of the angels turned to deeper colors and eventually to black. From light to dark, good to evil. Perfection to sin. From God to humanity.

Jennie had a hard time seeing Sean as the artist, especially one of this caliber, but then, she'd only just met him. "The guy definitely has talent."

"Jeremy," Declan's voice broke through Jennie's reverie. "Don't tell me you've decided to play hooky as well?"

"Okay, I won't." A guy about Jennie's age sauntered toward them, a sly grin on his face. "I thought since Sean and Shelagh thought these folks were worth staying home for, I should have a look too."

"Hmm." Declan didn't look pleased. "We'll talk later." His annoyance faded as he turned back to being a gracious host. "Jeremy, this is Helen Bradley and her granddaughter Jennie McGrady."

"Mrs. Bradley, Jennie." He nodded briefly, reminding Jennie of a dignitary. Jeremy looked like a prince—or what she imagined a prince would look like. He had sandy hair and a handsome face, and a smile graced his mouth and reached his eyes as he greeted her with the same slight nod. "Very nice to meet you both."

It was an act, Jennie decided. And he was getting a kick out of performing. Something in his eyes and the way he smiled at her set her instincts on edge. She wasn't sure why, but she didn't quite trust him. She'd felt that way with Sean too. Odd.

"Perhaps we should show the ladies to their rooms." Though gracious about it, Declan seemed anxious to move them along. Jennie suspected he had other things to do.

Jennie bent over to pick up a bag.

"Leave them," William said. "I'll have one of the servants bring them up."

Servants. Jennie shouldn't have been surprised.

She took another look at the ceiling and then headed up the winding marble staircase with the others. At the third floor the staircase opened into a long hallway with four doors on either side and one at the end. "You have the room at the end, Jennie." William pointed down the hallway but stopped before reaching it. "Helen, we've put you in here. There's a connecting suite between the rooms."

"It's like a hotel." Jennie stepped back as William opened the door to Gram's room and beckoned her inside. *Better than a hotel*, she thought. More like a master suite in a castle. Excitement bubbled through her again like an over-shaken soft drink. She suppressed the foaming joy and resisted the urge to dance around the room. She'd wait until she was tucked into her own room and out of sight of their hosts before cheering. The room was huge and held a fireplace and a double bed.

"It's wonderful." Gram moved to the window, where heavy, deep rose draperies had been opened to reveal a view of the grounds and the ocean some fifty yards away. An Oriental rug covered the polished wood floors. The furnishings were all antique and looked very expensive.

"Wow!" Jennie exclaimed, barely able to take it all in. "Are all your rooms like this?"

"Not yet," Declan said. "We've finished all of the rooms in this wing, though this floor didn't really need a lot of renovating. Dad turned the castle into a bed-and-breakfast for a time."

William cleared his throat and in an apologetic tone explained, "Money was a scarcity after World War II. Had to do something to put food on the table. Costs a lot of money to keep up a place like this. We did have the money my father left us, but spending it would have left us penniless within a few years. After talking it over with my mother and Declan, I decided to put the place to work for us. People seemed to love the idea of staying in a castle, particularly one so close to the ocean."

Gram slipped an arm through William's and beamed up at him. "No need for apologies."

"Yes, well, my mother wasn't too keen on the idea. My father wouldn't have minded—he'd have done the same thing. But Grandfather . . . it's his voice I hear in my head, telling me I'm lowering the Kavanagh standards. Guess I still feel a bit guilty."

"No need, Dad." Declan seemed annoyed that his father would bring the matter up. "You made a wise financial decision. It brought us out of the red and into the black again, by some distance. Come on, Jeremy, let's show Jennie to her room. Hate to rush you folks, but I have some phone calls to make."

"Go ahead, son," William offered. "Jeremy and I can take care of our guests."

Declan thanked him. "I'll leave you, then. We'll be having dinner at seven-thirty, Dad. Thomas said he couldn't be here any sooner. And that will give Helen and Jennie a chance to rest." Turning to Gram, he said, "I'll see you at dinner."

"You'll have to excuse the boy," William said when the door closed. "He's always busy." He sighed. "But then, as he says, it takes a lot of money to live here. And making money takes time."

Jeremy scowled. "It doesn't have to. We could turn it back into a B and B. Just because—"

William settled a hand on Jeremy's shoulder. The action ended the discussion.

"Jennie." William turned back to her. "I think you'll enjoy your room as well. Let's go through the sitting room so you can see the layout of the place. There's a common bath just off the sitting room." He stopped at the door to the bathroom, which had been done in tiles and had a huge old-fashioned bathtub as well as a more modern shower stall.

Luxury, Jennie thought, *pure luxury*.

William checked his watch. "Have you had lunch?"

"No," Gram answered. "I'm not hungry. But maybe Jennie would like something."

"It's no bother, really. I know you must be tired, so I'll have Megan bring a lunch tray."

After they left, Jennie squealed and fell back on the bed. "Isn't it fantastic?!"

"It's lovely. But I don't know where you get all that energy." Then she offered a knowing smile. "Aha. You got a nap in the car, didn't you?"

Without waiting for Jennie's response, Gram excused herself, saying she wanted to wash up and take a short nap.

"What about lunch?" Jennie asked. "Are you going to eat with me?"

"Um. I don't think I'll have anything just yet. Maybe after I wake up I'll go to the kitchen and scrounge up something."

Jennie nodded. "I'll probably eat enough for both of us."

Jennie bounced off the bed and twirled around in the center of the room. Lisa would have been even more thrilled than she. The room couldn't have been more perfect—smaller than Gram's but just right for Jennie. William had called it the turret room, so named for the rounded part of the room that displayed a panoramic view of the ocean and the long expanse of the estate, all the way to the house Gram used to live in. At the farmhouse Jennie could see a man, most likely Thomas, stroll from the barn and stop at the porch to remove his boots before going inside.

In front of the windows was a window seat, and Jennie tried it out, imagining herself sitting there reading or writing in her journal. In a small way it reminded her of her own room at home, but this one had been decorated in soft floral pastels. Outside, a tree gently tapped its highest branches against the window as though wanting to come in. Jennie opened the window a crack to let in some fresh air.

The cloudless sky they'd arrived to had turned to a steely gray. In the distance Jennie could see the faint glimmer of sunlight. She was facing west and would be able to watch the sunset from her room. Back in Oregon she had watched a hundred sunsets at the beach where Gram lived. How similar the Atlantic was to the Pacific—at least here on the western coast of Ireland. Jennie found it hard to believe that home was half a world away.

Jennie eyed her unpacked suitcases still on the floor. The elusive servant must have brought them while they were all in Gram's room. Jennie reluctantly pushed herself up from the comfortable seat to put her clothes away in the closet and antique chest of drawers. She was just stashing her shoes in the closet when someone knocked on the door.

Jennie opened it and stood face-to-face with a young woman holding a tray. "I've brought you some lunch."

"Thanks." Jennie reached for it, but the maid swerved around her and placed the tray on a table near the window.

"It's no trouble at all." She smiled. "I'm Megan. I'll leave you be for now, but if you need anything, anything at all, just ring me. There's an intercom there by the door." Megan turned to go. "Oh, and when you've finished with the tray, you can set it in the hallway. Mr. Kavanagh said you'd probably be wanting a bit of a nap."

"Um—thanks. You can stay . . ."

Megan turned and was out the door before Jennie finished the sentence. Jennie shrugged, went into the bathroom to wash her hands, and then tackled the generous lunch of a chicken salad sandwich and fresh fruit.

Weariness caught up to her then, and after setting the tray outside the door, Jennie sank onto the soft mattress and fell asleep.

———

Six hours later, Jennie meandered into the bathroom to wash up. She had to laugh at her image in the ornate gold-framed mirror. The face looking back at her looked tired but deliriously happy. Jennie sighed. Taking a washcloth from a brass ring, she soaked it in hot water and washed the grime of a day's travel from her face. The hot, wet cloth felt so good, she filled the old tub, splashed in a cap of bubble bath her hosts had provided, and after stripping off her clothes, eased into the steamy water. Sinking in until only her head remained above the water and bubbles, Jennie took several long and deep breaths, luxuriating in the silken feel of the bath and wondering what it would be like to own a castle.

Did Jeremy realize how lucky he was? A picture of him drifted into her mind.

"I doubt it," she commented aloud. Though she'd had no time to really get to know him, she'd noticed a couple of things about him. He wasn't very happy. He'd been pleasant enough, but not really happy. And he seemed arrogant. Maybe it was his age. She supposed she seemed sullen at times too. But not now. At this very moment she couldn't be happier.

Well, except that the nasty threat and the reality that someone out there meant to harm Gram still clouded Jennie's mind. But she wouldn't allow herself to think about that—not just now. They were safe here. The castle was a fortress, built to keep out the enemy.

But what if the enemy is inside?

Jennie ignored her errant thoughts and stayed in the tub, dreaming about life in the castle. She'd either have to make a lot of money or marry a man who did. Or maybe she'd inherit one. Gram owned a castle in the San Juan Islands. Her eccentric and very wealthy uncle Paddy, Mary's brother, had left Gram one-third of his estate and the rest to his two children. After Gram's own father, Hugh, had died when she was two, Uncle Paddy took over the father-figure role. Gram hadn't said much about Paddy's death, only that he had been poisoned. Maybe that was why she seemed so sad now. She could be thinking of poor Uncle Paddy and missing him. Her owning a castle would explain why she didn't share Jennie's enthusiasm about being in one now.

Jennie hadn't been to Gram's castle yet. She'd only

seen pictures, but the family planned to stay for three weeks this coming summer. Gram's castle was haunted—well, not really, but there was a cool story about a woman who had waited for her husband to return from the sea. He never had, and rumor was she still waited.

Jennie bet this castle had a lot of exciting stories attached to it as well. Tonight after dinner, she'd have to ask. She laughed at her mind's meanderings. What an imagination she had.

After her bath, Jennie wrapped the large, thick terry towel around herself and padded across the sitting room. She twisted the handle to open the door and at the same time raised her other fist to knock. The door drifted open a couple inches. She paused when a knock came from the main door. Gram went to open it. Though Jennie couldn't see the visitor, she recognized William's voice.

"You look lovely as always, Helen. Hope I'm not intruding."

"Of course not." Gram stepped back. "Come in. We're not late for dinner, are we?"

"Not at all. I just wanted a chance to speak with you privately." William closed the door and lowered himself into a chair not far from where Jennie stood—rooted to the floor, eavesdropping. She felt a moment's guilt before deciding not to close the door and leave the two adults to themselves. Jennie couldn't say what prompted her. Something in William's demeanor, maybe. More than likely, though, it was her curiosity.

"Is something wrong?" Gram asked.

"Yes and no. You see, Helen, one of the reasons I insisted you stay at the castle . . . that is . . . I was hoping you would do me a favor."

Gram laughed. "Of course I will. What is it?"

He raised an eyebrow. "Just like that? You aren't even going to ask me what it's about before saying yes?"

"I trust you, William. I doubt very much you'd ask me to do something illegal or—"

"Dangerous?" He hesitated. "Yes, well, that's the thing, isn't it. It could be dangerous. Though I suspect enough time has passed."

"What is it? Don't keep me in suspense."

William sighed. "My father."

"Liam?"

"Yes."

"But he's been dead for what—fifty years?"

"Fifty-five. Do you remember how he died, then?"

Gram shook her head. "I'm sorry, I don't."

"It wasn't talked about much. Oh, there are still stories floating about. Especially when it comes to his ghost."

"His ghost." Gram sank onto the bed. "I haven't heard about that in ages. You don't really believe. . . ?"

"What I believe is that my father's memory haunts the castle. Maybe the haunting is only in my own heart, my longing for a resolution. I was a young lad when he died—only three. I was told he fell from the watch walk atop the east tower during a terrible winter storm."

"How dreadful."

"Yes. But I've taken to walking the towers, and there's no way the man could have fallen. The walls are waist high and a foot thick. Apparently there were no witnesses—no one who's come forward, at least. Helen, I think he was murdered."

8

Jennie couldn't have moved now for anything. A dozen questions flitted through her head. Her heart hammered with excitement. Could William's request have anything to do with the threat? Had he told someone, and now that someone was trying to keep Gram from looking into the investigation?

"Murdered." Gram repeated the word and then—as if she were drawing him out—waited.

"What other answer could there be? I suppose it's possible that he jumped. Maybe it's even more likely. But I can think of no reason the man would commit suicide. He had a wife and son. . . ." William lowered his head and covered his eyes.

Gram went over to him and placed a hand on his shoulder. "I'm sorry."

"Foolish of me to be so emotional about it after all these years. But these past few months I can't seem to think of anything else. I'm a grown man—a grandfather— yet I can't seem to get past the pain of a little boy losing his father." He raised his head; tears glistened in his eyes. "Was life so terrible that he had to kill himself? Was it something I did or didn't do?"

"William . . ."

William took Gram's hand and held it. "I know. Children are not to blame for their parents' choices. But don't you see? I have to know the truth, Helen. And with your knowledge and training, I thought perhaps you could look into it."

"Oh, Willie. I don't know."

"Please. I'll pay you. Anything you want."

"No, you won't. I can't accept money from you." Gram sighed. "I'll look into his death, but I don't know what I can do. It's been so long."

William stood and pulled Gram into an embrace. "I've faith in you." He stood back. "Now I'd best leave so you can finish getting ready. I'll see you at dinner."

Gram's concerned gaze followed him out the door. When he'd gone, she cut across the room to the vanity and sat down in front of the mirror.

"You can come in now, Jennie."

"I . . ." Jennie eased open the door and stepped into the room. "I . . . I mean, how did you know I was there?"

"Elementary, my dear Watson. The door was closed earlier."

"I'm sorry. I didn't mean to eavesdrop. I was just coming to—" Gram's knowing look stopped her. "I was curious. I meant to leave, but when William said his father had been murdered, I had to hear the rest. I'm glad you're going to investigate."

"Hmm. I don't have much hope of finding anything. I can check the records and talk to people around town. Though truth and stories are often hard to differentiate— especially after all these years. Ireland is full of story-tellers—folks who like nothing better than to embellish their tales."

"But you'll look into it. You said you would."

"And I will."

"Can I help?"

"We'll see. I'll talk further with William about it in the morning, get as many details as I can."

Gram stood up, and for the first time since she'd come into the room, Jennie took a good look at her grandmother. "Wow. William was right. You do look gorgeous."

The deep rose wool dress showed off Gram's slender figure and hung in soft folds around her legs. She wore what was probably a garnet and diamond necklace and was putting in delicate matching earrings that dangled and caught the light as she moved.

"Thank you. Um . . ." Gram eyed Jennie's towel. "You might want to wear a dress, sweetheart. I understand that dinners here are usually formal."

Jennie giggled. "You don't like my towel? I thought it had a rather, um . . . flashy look."

"Well, white *is* your color," Gram teased.

"Actually, I wanted to ask you what I should wear. I guess jeans are out."

"Way out. Come on, I'll help you find something suitable."

Gram stopped to slip into a pair of black dress shoes with two-inch heels and followed Jennie through the suite into Jennie's room.

"Gram, do you think maybe that threat you got in the mail has anything to do with this?"

"With what?" Gram pulled something from the closet—a royal blue knit sleeveless turtleneck dress with a matching lightweight jacket.

"The investigation into Liam's death." Jennie slipped the dress off the hanger.

"It's possible. I haven't mentioned the threat to Willie yet. He may have some ideas."

"I thought maybe if he'd said something to someone . . ."

"A distinct possibility." Gram smiled.

Several minutes later, Jennie took one last look in the mirror. She looked and felt like a princess. Jennie didn't dress up much but loved it when she did.

She'd swept her hair up in a knot at the top of her head, letting several errant tendrils curl along the sides and back. Gram helped her secure a single gold and pearl necklace around her throat.

At seven-twenty-five sharp the two of them headed downstairs. William, dressed in a formal black suit and tie, greeted them as they entered the great hall. He gave no indication he and Gram had talked earlier as he beamed at Gram and bent to kiss the back of her hand. Though he'd been friendly with her before, now the action caused an odd flutter in the pit of Jennie's stomach. She thought of J.B. and what he might feel if he knew his wife was being so outwardly admired by another man. Jennie half expected Gram to remind him that she was married, but she didn't. In fact, she acted like she enjoyed his attentions. Jennie pinched her lips together. She would have to have a talk with her grandmother.

"Jeremy, my lad." William motioned to his grandson. "Be a gentleman and help me escort our guests." Turning to Jennie, he said, "You both look lovely tonight."

Jennie flushed. "Thanks."

"Our guests have already arrived," William said.

Jeremy, dressed in a suit as well, seemed reluctant about escorting her, but like a soldier obeying a command, he dutifully offered Jennie his arm. She watched William do the same for Gram and waited until they'd taken a few steps. To Jeremy she murmured, "This is weird. You don't have to escort me. I mean, it's not like we're going to a prom or anything."

He offered a genuine smile. "Yes, I do. Granddad likes to do things the old way. Dad plays along. You get used to it after a while."

Jennie shrugged. *You are in a castle, after all*, she told herself. The Keegan clan was already seated along the extended banquet table. Jeremy seated Jennie next to Catherine and sat down between Jennie and Shelagh. The remaining chair at the end of the table was still empty.

"Shall I check on Dad?" Jeremy asked William.

"No need." Declan walked in, made a slight bow to his guests, and eased into the chair. "Sorry to keep you waiting. I had some urgent matters to clear up." He'd changed into a tweed dinner jacket and tie but still wore the khaki slacks he'd worn earlier.

Declan slipped the maroon dinner napkin from the wine goblet and placed it on his lap. "Glad you could make it, Thomas. You didn't seem so certain when we spoke earlier. How's Molly doing?"

"Ah, herself is doing well enough. Birthed twins, she did. Both healthy, I might add."

"Glad to hear it."

"Who's Molly?" Jennie glanced from one to another.

"One of Da's best milkers, she is." Shelagh beamed. "I watched the birthing. Such a fine sight."

"That it was," Thomas agreed.

Shelagh turned to Jennie. "I was all for coming to fetch you so you could see it too, but Da said next time. Ye can come see the babes in the morning, though. Sean and I will be in school, but—"

"Shelagh," her father warned. "Mind your manners, now. Remember what your mum told you about monopolizing the conversation."

Shelagh gave Jennie a look of pure exasperation. Jennie grinned at her and said, "I'd like to see Molly's babies."

Before they had a chance to discuss Molly more, Megan bustled in from the kitchen and set to filling glasses and cups with desired beverages.

"Where's the duchess?" Bridget looked around the table. "Is she not joining us?"

Jennie perked up. "Duchess?"

"Not feeling well this evening," Declan answered. "She's taking dinner in her room." Turning to Jennie, he added, "The duchess is my grandmother. You'll meet her tomorrow if she's up to having visitors. She sends her apologies."

"I hope it's nothing serious," Gram said.

William patted her hand. "Just a flare-up of arthritis."

"Is she really a duchess?" Jennie asked, wondering if the duchess was the mysterious person who'd been watching them from the second-floor window when they arrived.

"She is." Declan offered a gracious smile. "Imported from England by my grandfather Liam Kavanagh."

Declan waited until the soup and bread were served and then, at Jennie's insistence, went on with his story. "As you've undoubtedly heard, many marriages were arranged back then. The duchess wasn't too happy about it. She apparently had no wish to come to Ireland to marry Liam, regardless of his stature. But marry him she did." Declan winked. "Truth be told, I think she really loved the man. My father was born a year later."

"It must have been difficult giving up England for Ireland," Bridget said. "We were a wild bunch then—all the wars going on, even if the Brits did cause them."

"Aye," William answered. "To her fine upbringing, Ireland must have seemed like hell itself, with all the fighting and such."

"She eventually adjusted to living here," Declan went on. "When Liam died only three years after my father was born, she stayed on and took care of Liam's father."

"And me, of course," William added. "Heart of gold, she has. And the perseverance of a saint. I was too young to remember much about him, but as I understand it, Grandfather was not an easy man to care for."

Jennie leaned forward, more curious than ever. The duchess had been Liam's wife, and if Liam had been murdered, she would be one of the first people Gram questioned. "You must have known her too, Gram."

"I did." Gram's voice sounded flat. She turned her attention to the soup in front of her. Jennie had the distinct impression that maybe the duchess wasn't quite as wonderful as William and Declan made her out to be. She sat back, determined to ask Gram about it later. This place was getting more interesting all the time.

"Sean." Gram aimed her gaze at him, obviously changing the subject. "I am thrilled to see you are pursuing your art studies. Your painting in the foyer is true genius."

Sean's cheeks flushed. Ducking his head to break a piece of bread, he said, "Thank you, ma'am." His gaze slanted toward his father.

"Aye." Bridget beamed at her son. " 'Tis a fine piece of work. He's a talent, no doubt."

Thomas raised an eyebrow. "Don't be giving the boy a big head, now. He's living in a dream world, he is, thinking he can paint pretty pictures for a living. I'll not be denying him his dreams so long as he—" Either he caught the stern look on Aunt Catherine's face or Bridget kicked him under the table, because he cleared his throat and added, "Makes a good wage."

"And he's made a good start at that, hasn't he, now," Catherine said. "Earning his way through art school, and him only sixteen."

"I suppose he has, at that."

After an uncomfortable silence, Thomas commented on how good the soup, a lobster bisque, was. Jennie finished hers just as Megan brought in the main course: roast beef with potatoes, gravy, and green beans.

"Mmm. This looks wonderful," Gram said.

Others murmured their agreement.

"Mum, can we stay home from school tomorrow so we can visit with Jennie?" Shelagh sliced into her meat and speared a piece with her fork. "Please?"

"No, you cannot. We've been through this before, luv. You'll not be missing any more school. I'm sure Jennie will find plenty to keep her occupied while you're gone."

Shelagh sighed. "Could she come to school with me, then? Sister Anna wouldn't mind. She told me Jennie was more than welcome."

Jennie paused with her forkful of mashed potatoes a few inches from her mouth. She didn't want to go to Shelagh's school. In some ways it might have been fun, but she had other plans—which now included a murder investigation she couldn't say anything about. And finding out who'd sent Gram the threat. How could she get out of it without hurting her cousin's feelings?

Sean smirked. "Now, do you really think she'll be wanting to spend her vacation in school?"

"It was a nice thought," Jennie finally spoke up. "I appreciate the invitation, Shelagh, really, but I have schoolwork to do myself. And I want to spend time with my grandmother and Aunt Catherine. We'll have plenty of time after school and on weekends." Seeing the disappointment in her cousin's green eyes, she added, "Maybe I'll come visit one day next week."

"That would be fine. Everyone in my class is wanting to meet you."

"Well, that's settled, then," Bridget said.

"Will you be up to some sight-seeing tomorrow, Helen? I'd love to take you to the horse races if you've a mind to go," William asked.

"The races? Dad, they just got here. The flight's a grueling one. I would imagine Helen and Jennie would both like to rest and catch up on their sleep."

"Thank you, Declan. I think we'll both want to sleep in. But . . ." Gram placed a hand on Catherine's. "We'll want to spend some time at the house. Catherine and I have a lot of catching up to do."

"And whose fault is that?" Catherine's voice was sharp, but her eyes sparkled in delight.

"I was hoping you would," Bridget said. "Why don't the two of you come for lunch, around eleven. That will give you time to sleep in, and I should have most of the chores done by then."

That decided, Declan and Thomas went on to talk about the farm. William, Catherine, and Gram talked in low tones, and Jennie could only pick up a word here and there, none of which really made sense. When they'd finished eating a lemon cream pie, Declan suggested they all go into the living room.

"I trust you brought your fiddle, Thomas." William settled an arm across the younger man's broad shoulders.

"That I did. My fingers 'ave been itching to play all evening."

"Wouldn't be an evening out without your fine music." William winked at Jennie. "The Irish love their music, lass. We'll be dancing and singing till the wee hours of the morning."

"Not quite that long." Bridget laughed. "The children have school tomorrow."

Shortly after the music started, Declan excused himself, saying he had to finish up some work and had errands to attend to the next day. Both Jeremy and William urged him to stay, but he insisted his work wouldn't wait.

Catherine, sitting on one of four sofas, reached into her bag and pulled out some fabric and began stitching two pieces together. Gram asked to see the pieces, and Catherine displayed a quilt block. It had pastel prints sewn in a fan shape.

"It's going to be lovely, but then, yours always are."

Catherine smiled and leaned over to whisper something in Gram's ear. A wide grin spread across Gram's face as she nodded in approval.

Jennie settled herself between Sean and Jeremy, and soon they were all listening to Shelagh sing Irish ballads. Shelagh's voice was as near perfect as any Jennie had ever heard. Clear and sweet, it had a haunting quality.

Jennie leaned toward Jeremy. "She's good enough to be making records."

"She is. Dad's looking into signing her on with the recording studio he owns part interest in."

Jennie followed his gaze as it fastened on Shelagh and stayed there. Jeremy liked Shelagh, Jennie decided. The thought made her smile.

After the singing came the dancing. Though Jennie had been practicing her Irish jig before coming, she felt as awkward as a two-legged stool. Shelagh, Sean, and Bridget moved across the floor, their upper bodies hardly moving while their feet seemed to fly. Jennie had seen the Irish dance troupes perform in concert in Portland and had loved them. Seeing her own cousins gave her an even greater thrill. She loved the rhythm and almost made it through an entire song before stumbling to the sidelines and plopping down beside Jeremy.

"I'm done," Jennie panted. She considered herself athletic, but this energetic dancing was like running a mile. "That's hard work."

Jeremy grinned at her. "You're brave to try. You have to remember, they've been dancing like this all their lives."

"It shows. I had no idea my cousins were so talented."

At ten that evening, Thomas stopped his fiddling and announced it was time for his family to go home. William seemed disappointed but cheerful as he helped them gather their coats.

"I'll see you after school, then, Jennie," Shelagh said as the others went out. "We've planned a picnic—Sean, Jeremy, and I—so we can show you about."

"Do you ride, Jennie?" Jeremy asked.

"Some."

Sean grinned. "Good. We'll take the horses and go out on the cliffs."

"Great."

Shelagh's eyes took on a mischievous glow. "I'll be making my special cookies."

"That sounds good too." Jennie didn't understand how a person could get that excited over making cookies. But whatever. Shelagh was up to something. Come to think of it, so were the boys. She hadn't missed the smug looks that had passed between the two of them. Then again, maybe she was just imagining things. She tended to have a suspicious nature anyway, and the threat to Gram didn't help. Not that Jennie suspected her cousins or Jeremy of foul play. There'd be no reason for them to want Gram out of the picture. Or would there?

Just as Thomas opened the door, Declan ran down the stairs toward them, frowning. "There's a fire!" he gasped. "At your house, Thomas. I saw the flames from my study."

9

The temperature had dropped twenty degrees, and a thick mist had rolled in from the ocean. Wishing she'd taken time to get a jacket before going to the farmhouse, Jennie shivered and wrapped her arms around herself. Tired and stunned, she watched the taillights of the fire truck disappear. The fire was out, and damage to the house was minimal.

Like the others, Jennie had prayed it would be.

The fire had been purposely set. Fortunately, recent rains had soaked the house and surrounding area. The flames Declan had seen from the castle had been gasoline-soaked rags that had flared up and burned themselves out. They were stumped as to who might want to burn them out and why.

Jennie went inside with the rest of the family and the Kavanaghs. William and Declan were trying to talk the Keegans into coming to the castle to spend the night.

"Thanks for the offer, but we'll be fine here," Thomas insisted.

"Well, in that case, perhaps we'd best get back." William sighed. "If you change your mind . . ."

Thomas shook his head. "We won't."

Jennie expected Shelagh to object, but she had become uncharacteristically quiet. Jennie couldn't blame her. Having someone try to set your house on fire was a sobering thing. Frightening as well.

Jennie hugged her. "I'm sorry, Shelagh. I'll see you tomorrow?"

Shelagh nodded. Tears gathered in her eyes.

"Will you still want to go riding tomorrow?" Jeremy asked.

Shelagh and Sean both looked at their parents, who now stood arm in arm. "I don't . . . "

"There's no reason you shouldn't go on as usual," Thomas said.

Sean grinned. "It's set, then."

They said their good-byes and headed outside.

"Where are you off to, Jeremy?" Declan asked when Jeremy started down the path to the beach instead of going to the car.

"You've got a full load. I need a run. Jennie, would you like to come with me?"

"Um, thanks for the offer, but I don't have my jacket." Besides, Jennie wanted to talk to Gram about the fire.

Jeremy shrugged and took off running.

"Gram, could the fire somehow be connected with the threat you got?" Jennie asked as they walked out to the car. "Maybe the person who sent it thought we were staying at the farm."

"Mmm. I thought about that myself, but there's one problem. The dog. Gracie never would have allowed a stranger to come into the yard. You saw how she was with the firemen. If she'd have raised that much of a ruckus, we'd have heard her clear over at the castle."

"Maybe the arsonist gave her some food." Jennie climbed into the backseat after Gram.

Gram frowned. "No, I think Thomas is right. Whoever set that fire was someone Gracie knew and trusted. Besides that, we weren't there. No one was home. I really doubt the fire was meant to harm us."

"They weren't very bright, that's for certain," Declan put in from the front seat.

William agreed. "At least not very serious about it.

With everything so wet still, any idiot would know you'd need more than a few douses of gasoline to start a fire big enough to burn down the house."

Gram took hold of Jennie's hand. "You may be right in thinking there's a connection. Perhaps the fire was meant to frighten us. I'm sure the police will get to the bottom of it."

Jennie leaned her head back against the seat and yawned. "I hope so."

Declan dropped Jennie, Gram, and William off at the front door and headed back to the garage.

Jeremy came around the corner of the house. Jennie waited for him while Gram and William went inside. When Jeremy reached the steps, he bent over, resting his hands on his knees. "Whew, good run. Tide's out. You should have come with me."

Jennie rubbed her arms. "It's freezing out here." She opened the front door to go inside.

Jeremy placed a hand on her arm. "What do you make of it, Jen?"

"What do you mean?"

"The fire. You must have some idea. Shelagh's always going on about how you solve all these crimes. So are you going to solve this one?"

Jennie shrugged. "I . . . I don't know where to start. All I know is that Gram got a note telling her to stay out of Ireland. Then, we no sooner leave the airport than she's nearly run over. And now, the place where we were planning to stay is set on fire."

"Makes you wonder, doesn't it? Well, I'd best get upstairs. School tomorrow. As it is, my brain will be mush from lack of sleep."

Jennie nodded. "Mine too, but at least I get to sleep in."

Jennie watched Jeremy bound up the stairs and then stood in the entry a moment. She was about to head up to her room when she heard voices coming from the sitting room. Gram and William were sitting side by side on one of the sofas, apparently deep in conversation. Were they talking about the murder? They looked up as Jennie entered.

"Oh, hi, sweetheart." Gram held a hand out to her. "I thought you'd gone up to bed. Did you need something?"

"Um . . . not really."

"We were just going to have some tea to settle our nerves. Would you like some?"

Jennie shook her head. The tea sounded good, but bed sounded better. "I was just going up to bed."

"Good idea. I'll be up shortly." Holding out an arm, Gram said, "Come give me a good-night kiss."

Jennie reached down to hug her and kiss her cheek.

"See you in the morning." Jennie turned to William. "Good night."

"Sleep well, lass."

Jennie took her time walking out of the room into the foyer and up the stairs. She could hear nothing but a soft murmur of voices. Were they talking about William's father, the fire, or both? Maybe Gram would fill Jennie in the next day. Maybe Jennie should have stayed and had tea with them.

When she got to the second floor, Jennie couldn't remember which floor she and Gram were on. She thought she recognized a painting and started toward the end of the hall. About halfway down the hall, she heard voices. Angry voices came from behind a set of carved wooden doors.

"Don't give me that garbage," Jeremy yelled. "You don't care about me. All you ever do is work."

"I work to keep food on the table and you in school." Declan matched him decibel for decibel. "It takes a lot of hours to run a business."

"I don't care. I liked it better when we lived in the apartment in New York. I never wanted to come here."

"Jeremy . . ." Declan sounded tired.

"I want to go home. Mom wants me. At least—"

"This *is* your home. You are not going back to the States."

"This is *your* home, not mine. I talked to Mom this afternoon. She and Tom are buying a house. She says there's an extra room."

"We'll talk about it later." Declan sounded hoarse.

"There's nothing to talk about. I'm sixteen. I can make my own decisions."

"No, you can't. Jeremy—"

One of the doors opened and Jeremy burst out, nearly colliding with Jennie.

He muttered a curse and closed the door behind him. Grabbing her arm, he led her farther down the hall before confronting her.

"Ouch. That hurts." She wrenched her arm from his grasp.

"Sorry." He scowled at her. "What are you doing here?"

"I . . . I was going to my room."

"Right. You're on the wrong floor."

"Sorry, I didn't know. I couldn't remember."

"It's okay." Jeremy lightened up. "It's easy to get lost here. Come on. I'll take you to your room."

She touched his arm as they walked back toward the stairs. "Jeremy?"

"What?"

"Are you okay?"

"Does it look like it?" he snapped. Then he sighed, dragging a hand through his hair. "I'm sorry. It's nothing to do with you. Dad's being a total jerk."

"I heard you say you were going to live with your mom."

"He doesn't want me to. He thinks she doesn't want me. That's not true. Yeah, she's got another family, but I'm still her son."

"How long have they been divorced?"

Jeremy shrugged. "Six years. Been living with Dad most of the time. Sometimes, when we lived in the States, I'd see my mom on weekends and for a couple of weeks in the summer."

"So your dad has custody?"

"It's a joint-custody thing. Mom was a flight attendant and traveled a lot. It was easier staying with Dad. But she's married and has a house now—in California."

They reached the staircase, and Jeremy indicated they needed to go up another flight to the third floor.

"Are you really leaving?"

"Yeah. As soon as my mother sends me a ticket."

"Hmm. It must be hard having your parents in two different places."

"Yeah."

"Do you have any brothers and sisters?" Jennie hurried to catch up to him.

"No—at least, I didn't until Mom got married. She's got a three-year-old and a baby."

Jennie winced. "She's kind of starting over, huh?"

"Yeah. But she wants me there. Dad says she just wants a built-in baby-sitter."

"What a cruel thing to say." Jennie wondered if it was true. It seemed strange that his mother would wait until he was sixteen to invite him into her home. Jennie felt sad for him, but it really wasn't any of her business.

At the top of the stairs, Jeremy turned right and led Jennie down the hall to her door.

"I hope everything works okay for you—with your parents, I mean."

"It will. I've made up my mind to go. Dad's just going to have to accept that. Mom has every right to have me stay with her."

Jennie nodded, though she didn't necessarily agree. "I don't see how you can leave the castle, though." She smiled. "I'd love to live here."

"Wait till you've spent the night here. You may change your mind."

"Why's that?"

"The ghosts come out at night." Jeremy's voice took on an ominous tone, and though Jennie thought he was teasing her, she still felt goose bumps shiver up her arms.

"There are all kinds of them here," Jeremy went on. "Sometimes they'll go into their old rooms and play pranks on the people who are sleeping there."

Jennie straightened. "Jeremy, please. There are no ghosts. If you're trying to scare me, it isn't working." It was, but she had no intention of letting him know that.

He tossed her a crooked grin. "Don't worry. They're not dangerous. Haven't killed anybody yet, that I know of. Of course, it might have been a ghost that killed my great-grandpa Liam. He supposedly fell off the walk."

"The stairs ended at this one. I noticed there were five stories."

"There's another set of stairs. Two, in fact. But only one leads to the upper floor and the walkway. Soldiers used to stand guard up there all night during the battles. That's who you'll hear walking around up there at night, all the dead soldiers."

"Humph." The hair on the back of Jennie's neck stood on end. Still, she was not about to back down. "You're wasting your time trying to scare me. It isn't going to work. I'm immune." He was going to give her nightmares.

Looking into his eyes, Jennie realized that's exactly what he meant to do.

"Good night, Jeremy. Have fun with your ghosts. I'm going to sleep." She let herself in and took a quick look around before turning back to him.

Hands in his pockets, he cocked his head. "Sweet dreams," he drawled. Turning around, he started to make his way back down the hall. After a few steps he looked back. "I'd lock my door if I were you." Chuckling softly, he half jogged to the stairs and disappeared down the staircase.

Jennie told herself over and over that Jeremy had only been teasing. There were no ghosts in the castle. Still, Jeremy's tales and her own vivid imagination, along with the fact that someone didn't want Gram in Ireland, kept Jennie awake and shivering for well over an hour. She finally felt herself drifting off. A flash of light and crash of thunder brought her bolt upright. Something lashed against her window.

"It's just a storm," she said aloud, trying to calm her wild heart. Her breaths came in snatches as the window smashed open. A cold, wet wind swished through the room.

Two massive forms came toward her.

10

Jennie tried to scream, but nothing came out. She plunged under the covers.

Her immediate terror dissipated as she waited and nothing happened. Her heart stopped bouncing in her chest, and her breathing settled into its normal rhythm.

Okay. Just stay calm. Think.

There are no ghosts.

But you saw them. They were real. Dark and scary.

Replaying the scene in her mind, Jennie realized the vision, enhanced by only a dim night-light, had not been a ghostly apparition at all. It was the wind.

"Stop being so jumpy," she scolded herself for being such a coward. "Those ghosts were only the heavy drapes blowing in the wind." Hearing the explanation lessened Jennie's fears even more. Swallowing hard, she eased out from under the covers and pressed herself against the headboard, her heart racing again at the sight of the heavy curtains undulating in some strange unearthly dance. The scratching noise continued. Jennie remembered the tree branches just outside the window. Holding her breath, she tossed the comforter aside and went to the window, closed it, and securely fastened the latch. The drapes turned back into limp fabric, now damp from the rain.

She took a calming deep breath and leaned against the wall. "There is nothing to be afraid of." Even as she spoke, Jennie dove back into the bed and crawled under the covers. The tree continued its scratching at the window-pane. The wind howled. *There is nothing to be afraid of*, she told herself over and over again. Much as she wanted to believe it, she couldn't. What if Jeremy's sordid tale was true? What if Liam had been murdered by ghosts? What if those same ghosts were here now?

Stop it, McGrady. Stop it right now. It's the wind and nothing else. But there *was* something else. It seeped into Jennie's consciousness like ice water into a sponge, chilling her to the bone. The window had been closed when she'd gone to bed. Fear shrieked through her once again. Had someone been in her room to open it? She peeked out from under the blankets.

There has to be a reasonable explanation. Windows don't open themselves.

Maybe she hadn't secured the latch earlier and it had worked its way loose. *Of course. That's it. The latch was loose and the wind worked it open.*

Jennie forced herself to breathe slow, deep breaths. She was perfectly safe—a victim of her own imagination and Jeremy's spooky tales.

And a threatening note. And the fire.

The threat was aimed at Gram, not you.

Jennie slipped out of bed, went into the bathroom, and quietly opened the door to Gram's room. Gram's steady breathing reassured her. She thought for a moment of snuggling into bed with her but changed her mind. Gram needed her sleep.

Jennie returned to her room and crawled back into bed. They were safe. At least for now.

Still, the damage had been done. Jennie was wide awake, and even if the noises were coming from the storm, she'd never be able to relax enough to go back to sleep. To calm herself, Jennie did what she often did when she was afraid. She recited the Twenty-third Psalm over and over. " 'The Lord is my Shepherd. . . .' " She lost track of how many times she said it before finally drifting off.

Sunlight made a long, bright beam between the curtains. Jennie rolled over, getting caught up in the sheets. She put up her hand to block the bright light and groaned. "It's too early to get up."

She heard water running in the bathroom and Gram singing something about Irish eyes smiling. Jennie pulled up the covers and buried her head under them. She wasn't ready to get up and might never be. She must have fallen back asleep, because in what seemed to be the next moment, Gram was sitting on her bed, stroking her hair and telling her it was time to rise and shine.

"Come on, sleepyhead. It's ten o'clock already. We have to be at Aunt Catherine's in an hour."

Jennie groaned. "Do I have to go?"

"No. You can stay in bed the rest of the day if you'd like. Catherine will be disappointed, but she'll understand."

"I'll go." Jennie rolled over on her back and lifted one eyelid. Gram had opened the curtains to let even more light in. Jennie yawned and stretched. "I didn't sleep much last night."

"Hmm. Hard to sleep in a new place. I heard a few creaks and groans myself, but once I got to sleep I was out for the night. Didn't wake up until eight-thirty."

Jennie told Gram about her talk with Jeremy and her nighttime ordeal and how she thought someone had opened the window. Gram agreed that it probably had not been properly latched. "Jeremy shouldn't be frightening you like that."

Jennie sat up. "It's okay. I only half believed him. Even if he hadn't said anything, I'd have heard all the noises. No wonder people think the place is haunted." She glanced at the window again. "It is kind of spooky—especially at night."

"I'm sorry you were frightened. You could have come

into my room." Gram smiled. "Like you used to do when you'd have nightmares."

"I thought about it, but you were asleep."

Gram went over to the window.

"There aren't really ghosts living here, are there?" Jennie rubbed her eyes and yawned.

"Probably not. Most things associated with ghosts can be explained away. This place is centuries old. So full of history. It's possible that we can have a sense of those who lived before."

"Jeremy says a ghost killed his great-grandfather Liam. I know he was just trying to scare me, but . . ."

"I don't believe Liam was killed by a ghost."

"But the Bible talks about spirits and demons, so maybe . . ."

"It does. And I'll admit there are many things we can't explain. But the Bible tells us that the spirit of God living in us is stronger than any evil spirit we may encounter."

" 'Greater is he that is in you, than he that is in the world,' " Jennie quoted the verse.

"Exactly." Gram hugged her. "Now then, why don't you shower and get dressed. I'll meet you downstairs, and we'll walk over to the house together. We can take the beach route."

Once she'd showered, Jennie began to feel almost normal again. She couldn't believe how she'd let the wind frighten her that way. All houses had their share of noises, and castles apparently had more than most.

Jennie slipped on a T-shirt and jeans and topped them with a warm sweater. She towel-dried her hair and gathered it back in a French braid. By the time she was dressed, her tired feeling had subsided. She was in Ireland. She'd survived a night in a "haunted" castle. And she had a mystery to solve. Or maybe three.

Jennie was about to leave when someone knocked on the door.

"Oh, hi, Megan. I was just leaving."

Megan bustled in with a tray.

"Good morning, miss." She looked warm and flushed. "I trust you slept well. Your Gram said you'd be wanting a bite to eat before you leave, as you didn't make it down for breakfast."

"You didn't need to do that. I could have come downstairs."

"It isn't much. Just juice and a sweet roll. Something to tide you over until lunch."

Jennie shrugged. "Okay. Since you brought it . . ." She lifted the cover from the plate and picked up the orange juice.

"Well, then," Megan backed out. "Will you be needing anything else?"

"Some company would be nice. Why don't you sit down and talk with me?"

Megan bit her lip. "Oh, I shouldn't. Mum expects me to have the dusting done before noon."

"What's it like to work here? Do you like it?"

Megan's eyes widened. "I do. We're lucky to have such kind employers. Been here since I was twelve."

"Do you live here on the grounds?"

"Oh yes. There's an apartment on the other side. Very roomy."

"So your whole family works here?"

"There's just Mum, Da, and me. I've a brother, Kevin. He's away at college in Dublin. He works here too, in the summer."

"I think it would be great to have a job in a castle. Gram is part owner of one in the San Juan Islands. I might get to work there this summer. It's a resort."

"That's nice." Megan moved closer to the door. "I'd love to visit, Jennie, really I would. Maybe later, when me work's done. I should be getting back. Mum needs me in the kitchen."

"Sorry. I hope I didn't get you into trouble."

"Oh no. You didn't. It's just that we've a lot to do.

Mum's kitchen help quit last week, and we've been too busy to look for a replacement."

Jennie nodded in understanding. She quickly finished eating and hurried downstairs to meet Gram. Other than Megan and her parents—Beatrice and Mac—who were busy working, Gram and Jennie seemed to have the place to themselves.

William, Gram said, had gone into town to drink coffee and chat with some old friends.

The two of them left by the front door and circled around to the back of the house to the ocean side. There they took a well-worn path to the beach and walked along the cliff.

"Did you and William talk any more last night about the murder?" Jennie asked. "I noticed you were deeply engrossed in a conversation about something when I went to bed."

Gram hesitated. "A little. Mostly we talked about our childhood. We were inseparable as children, you know, much to our parents' chagrin. Neither my mother nor Willie's seemed to want us playing together. They were both proud and extremely class conscious."

"And you were Catholic and he a Prot."

Gram gave her a sideways glance. "Where did you hear that?"

"Shelagh told me Sean didn't trust Prots." Jennie shrugged.

"Mmm. I'd just as soon you didn't use that word. It feels disrespectful and insulting."

Jennie winced. "You're right. I'm sorry."

"I suppose I'm being overly sensitive. It shouldn't make any difference—whether we're rich or poor, of this religious persuasion or that. But to some people it does."

"And that's why you don't like the duchess?"

Gram seemed surprised. "Where did you get that idea?"

"Last night at dinner, I had the feeling you didn't."

"Well, I don't dislike her. It really wasn't her fault. Besides, my mother was just as opinionated. In some ways she was even more adamant about keeping Willie and me separated."

When they'd gone a few feet, Jennie ventured another question. "So if your parents didn't want you together, what did you do?"

"We'd meet here at the beach, go fishing as I'd mentioned. Other days we'd explore the forests. We were both rather wild and stubborn."

"Did you go out together when you were my age?"

"Not really. I suppose I wondered what it would be like to marry him. But William and I were never romantically involved. Though we both knew we'd never marry each other, I couldn't imagine not being with him. He was my best friend. Perhaps in some ways he still is."

"Sounds romantic to me. Why didn't you marry him?"

"Well, as you pointed out, I was a Catholic and he was a Protestant. His family was wealthy. We were very poor. My mother was adamant that William and I keep our relationship strictly platonic. I guess on some level we knew we'd never be more than friends. He married shortly after college."

"J.B. will be glad to hear that. I was a little worried last night."

Gram chuckled. "You were, were you? Well, you needn't worry, darling. J.B. is the love of my life." Gram gazed out at the water. "Did I ever tell you that J.B. and I knew each other in college?"

"I knew he was Grandpa Ian's best friend."

"Yes, and he became mine as well. As I look back now, I realize I was in love with him back then. I'd have married him if he'd asked."

"Then why did you marry Grandpa Ian? Didn't you love him?"

"As strange as it sounds, Jennie, I loved all three men—in different ways. Ian, J.B., and I were government agents, you know. I loved them both, but it was Ian who proposed. He seemed at the time to offer more stability. He wanted a family and a home. I wanted that as well." Gram frowned. "I struggled with my feelings for a while, wondering what to do. J.B. became distant and aloof. Only recently did I learn that he had loved me as well but didn't want to stand in Ian's way."

"Are you sorry you married Grandpa Ian?"

"Sorry? Heavens, no. It was a perfect match." She smiled. "Look what came out of our union, Jennie. Your father and your aunt Kate. You and Nick, Lisa and Kurt." Gram sighed and hung an arm around Jennie's neck. "No, darling. I wouldn't change a thing."

"It must be neat to have had so many guys in love with you."

"You should know. Look at the young men who flock around you."

Jennie grimaced. "I don't even have a boyfriend now. Scott's going out with a girl who shares his environmental interests. Ryan is dating Camilla. Eric's gone to California to Bible college. Every guy I meet turns out to be just a friend."

"Which is a good thing at your age. Eventually, in another ten years or so, you'll meet the right guy and you'll know."

"Ten years? I'll be twenty-seven."

"Which is the ideal age as far as I'm concerned. By then you'll be out of college and have a career."

Jennie smiled at the thought. She'd be a lawyer or a police officer or a detective. She wasn't certain which, but it would be in law enforcement.

"Did you know that Ryan broke up with Camilla?" Gram announced out of the blue.

Jennie's heart dropped to her shoes. "Really?"

Ryan Johnson was Gram's next-door neighbor and Jennie's long-time friend. Around her birthday last year they'd felt something deeper for each other—or thought they did until he met Camilla, a girl he went to school with. Jennie didn't blame him for liking her. Camilla had had a crush on him for a long time.

"Mmm. He came over the other day and asked what I thought about his calling you. He wanted to know if I thought you'd still be interested in going out with him."

Jennie winced. "What did you tell him?"

"To talk to you."

"He hasn't called."

"He knew you were coming to Ireland with me. Maybe he decided to wait until you got back."

"Or maybe he went back to Camilla." Jennie hoped not. Conflicting emotions chased around inside her. "Do you think I should go out with him?"

"What do you want to do?"

"Hit him." Jennie paused. "And hug him."

Gram laughed. "I don't blame you for wanting to hit him. But from what you've told me, Ryan has always been honest with you. He knows his dating Camilla hurt you, but he felt he had to discover his true feelings for her. If it's any consolation, he says he can't stop thinking about you. That's why he broke it off with Camilla."

Jennie bit her lips. "I keep thinking about him too. I've really liked Scott and Eric, but Ryan is . . . different. It's confusing."

"You certainly don't need to make a decision at this point. Just follow your heart and enjoy your friends."

They climbed down the rocks to walk along the shore, scattering a collection of gulls.

Jennie sighed. Would she take Ryan back if he asked? He'd been more than a jerk at times. And he'd hurt her. He'd always wanted to stay connected, though. How often had he told her their friendship was important to him? It was important to Jennie as well.

What do you think, God? Should I forgive him?

Jennie knew she would eventually. But at the moment

Ryan was an ocean away, and Jennie had far too many other things to think about.

"Gram, wait!" She scampered over the rocks to catch up. When she did, Jennie broached the subject of the threat again. "Aren't you worried?"

"I've given the note to the police. They're trying to find out who tried to run me down. I'm trying to come up with a logical solution, but there doesn't seem to be one. And I've given it over to the Lord. Not sure there's much else I can do but worry. And where would that get me?"

"Nowhere, I guess."

"Let's not worry over it. If something happens, we'll deal with it. Right now, I'm not going to let it spoil our trip. And I don't want you to worry over it either, okay?"

"I'll try. Um . . . are you still planning to send me home early?"

Gram sighed. "I don't know, Jennie. I'll talk to your parents—"

Gram's sentence went unfinished as they heard the crack of a gunshot. Gram dove to the sand, taking Jennie with her. "Stay down," she ordered as the blast came again.

11

Jennie didn't need to be told to stay down. She couldn't have moved if she'd wanted to. After a couple more pops and the revving of an engine, Gram scrambled to her feet. "My goodness. That thing is loud."

"What?"

"It was just a car backfiring."

Jennie followed Gram's gaze to an old pickup rumbling away from the docks. It fired off a couple more pings before disappearing over a ridge. "Are you sure? Sounded like someone was shooting at us."

Gram shook her head. "I should know the difference. Just jumpy, I guess."

Jennie could understand why. They had both been shot at a time or two, and the threatening letter indicated that someone might do it again.

Jennie got up on her knees, then her feet, brushing the sand out of her sweater and hair.

Gram clucked. "Should have known better than to think they were gunshots."

"It could have been for real."

"I know . . . the note."

"And whoever was driving that white van."

"I just can't imagine anyone not wanting me here in Ireland. I haven't made any enemies here that I know of."

"Except that William talked to you about his father being murdered. He could have told someone—"

"Jennie." Gram reached up to tuck an errant strand of hair behind Jennie's ear. "There's nothing to concern yourself with. If Liam was murdered, his killer would have to be nearly eighty. I really don't think we've anything to fear in that regard."

Jennie's mouth stretched into a smile. "I guess you're right."

"Helen, Jennie!" Thomas shouted as he bounded over the rocks near the dock. He jumped from the rocks onto the sandy beach. "Thought that was you." Approaching them, he looked from one to the other. "Are ye all right? I saw you fall."

"We're fine." Gram shook her head. "Mistook the backfire of that old truck for gunshots."

"Aye." Thomas shook his head. "Easy enough to do. Old Murphy should have buried that old eyesore years ago. Nothing but paper clips and elastics holding the old rattletrap together. Sorry he frightened you."

"No harm done."

"Well then, I'll let you be on your way. I take it you're going to the house to visit Catherine and Bridget."

"Yes." Gram glanced at her watch. "We decided to walk. Looks like we're late."

"No need to worry yourself about that. We're not for looking at clocks around here."

Gram smiled. "What brings you down to the docks?"

"Been fishing. It's a glorious day for it, wouldn't you say?"

"It is that."

They walked with Thomas across the short stretch of beach and climbed over the rocks and onto the dock.

"What kind of fish do you catch here?" Jennie asked.

"The usual saltwater fish—cod, snapper. Salmon's a favorite with my family. Caught a couple of nice ones today. If you care to see them, I'll show you my catch."

"Sure," Gram said. "Salmon's always been my favorite."

They followed him to the end of the dock and waited while he jumped aboard an old-style fishing boat. From the box in the back he lifted the lid and held up two salmon nearly his own size. "I'll sell one of them—the other we're having for dinner."

"Beautiful," Gram said. "It's been a long time since I've seen salmon that size."

"Bridget wants you to stay for dinner."

"I can never turn down salmon." Gram laughed. "However, if we don't get up to the house, Bridget may regret the invitation."

"No chance of that."

They hurried back to the platform and dock and up the gangplank toward the road. From there it was only a short distance to the house.

Catherine stood on the porch waving at them. "Saw you coming," she called. "Water's hot for tea."

Moments later they were all inside, sitting around the kitchen table exchanging pleasantries. They mostly talked about memories and family and discussed every branch in the O'Donnell family tree. By two-thirty, Jennie had heard enough talking to last her a year and didn't think she could sit still another minute.

During a lull in the conversation, Jennie took the opportunity to ask about Mary's things. "I know they're in the attic. Could I see them?"

"Getting bored, are you?" Bridget asked.

Jennie flushed. "I . . . ah . . . it's not that."

"It's about time someone took an interest," Catherine clipped, her gaze landing on Gram.

"Catherine . . ." Gram took another sip of tea as if for courage. "There's plenty of time. It's hard—" There was a catch in her voice.

"I know." Catherine's tone softened. "But there's a time for weeping and a time to run and a time to come home and face the past."

"Soon, Auntie." Turning to Jennie, Gram said, "You

can go up and look around if you'd like, Jennie. That is, if Catherine and Bridget don't mind."

"Not at all, lass," Catherine said. "I'd go up with you if I could. Just take the stairs straight up. There's a door at the landing that'll take you up to the attic. Ye'll find a candle on the small table."

"Should be matches there," Bridget added. "But just in case . . ." She paused and went to the fireplace to snatch a box off the mantel. "Take these with you. Bring them back, mind. I'm down to me last box. I've tried to keep things tidy, but undoubtedly you'll find a mass of cobwebs by now. Take care, Jennie. There's no railing around the stairwell up there."

"Why don't you come too, Gram?" Talk of candlelight and cobwebs was making Jennie nervous. She'd have loved some company.

"Not yet. I'll get to them eventually." Gram glanced back at Bridget. "I have to work myself up to it. Too many memories I'm not yet ready to face."

It had been three years since Mary's death. Jennie supposed it took some people longer to grieve than others. Maybe there was more to it all than grief. Gram seemed troubled about something. Jennie wondered if it might have had something to do with William. Had Gram been angry with Great-grandmother Mary for not letting her marry William? Had Gram been telling the truth about their just being friends? Of course she was. Gram had no reason to lie. Did she?

Jennie thanked Bridget and moved into the sitting room. Instead of going directly to the stairs, she paused at a dark-stained desk cluttered with papers. She glanced back at the kitchen. Gram, Catherine, and Bridget were still talking. Jennie looked over the papers, paying special attention to the handwritten notes. Nothing resembled the writing on the threat.

Relieved, Jennie made her way up the stairs, sliding her hand along the carved wooden banister—the same banister Gram had held on to when she was Jennie's age. At the landing Jennie found the candle Catherine had mentioned, lit it, and opened the narrow attic door. The hinges squeaked. Jennie hesitated and then moved through the doorway. Bridget was right about the cobwebs. Jennie's hand brushed several as she climbed the narrow stairs. Maybe it was a residual fear from the night before. Maybe it was the darkness that closed around her as the door behind her clicked shut. Jennie's heart thumped heavily in her chest. She crept up the remaining steps.

There are no ghosts here. Nothing to be afraid of.

The thought had no sooner entered her head than she heard a scurrying of tiny feet across the attic floor. *Mice.*

Just cute little mice who are terrified of you. The idea softened Jennie's fears but didn't allay them altogether. Maybe she should go back to the kitchen and wait until someone could come up with her. She didn't know why she wanted to look through an attic full of old stuff anyway.

Curiosity. Jennie lifted the candle higher and looked to the right and left. The room was low and long. The pitch of the roof allowed her to fully stand only in the center. On either side it sloped with the eaves of the house. As she stepped away from the stairs, she had to duck to keep from hitting her head on the exposed timbers. Once she'd cleared the stairs, Jennie set the candle on a large chest of drawers that had to be at least a hundred years old.

Narrow slats of light filtered into the room from the two ends. Air vents, Jennie decided.

What was she doing here? How was she supposed to look through this stuff when her only light was a dim candle?

The attic smelled dusty and a bit damp. Her eyes grew accustomed to the candlelight, allowing her to see more clearly. She pulled open the top drawer of the bureau on which she'd set the candle. Dust tickled her nose and made her sneeze.

Examining the contents of the drawer, Jennie was

pleased to find it filled with linens. Some of them she felt certain had been handmade by Mary herself. She pulled a neatly folded hanky out to admire its dainty lace trim. She folded it and put it back and then opened each of the drawers, all of them filled with linens: napkins, tablecloths, beautiful lace doilies. Jennie took a number of them out, examined them one by one, and neatly folded them again. In the bottom drawer Jennie's hand hit something hard. She removed several napkins and found a book. The pages were yellowed and worn. Opening the front cover, Jennie read, *Mary Elizabeth O'Donnell 1940.* The pages were of parchment and had been written by hand. A diary. Jennie felt a stirring of excitement. Mary would have been barely a woman then. Jennie opened the book.

As she began to read, she heard a click. The wind stirred and the candle went out.

12

"Jennie?" A sweet, lilting voice drifted up the stairwell. *Shelagh*. "I'm up here." Jennie knew she sounded breathless. The breeze and the candle going out had sent her heart rate into orbit. If she kept getting these scares, she was going to have to check herself into the cardiac unit of a local hospital.

"What are you doing up there in the dark?"

Jennie couldn't help but laugh. "I wasn't in the dark until you opened the door. The candle went out."

"I'm sorry. Do you have matches? Shall I bring another candle?"

"No need. I can relight it." Jennie felt around on the dresser top where she'd set the matches, selected a match, and struck the side of the box. The flame flickered as she relit the candle.

"Mum says you've been up here for nearly an hour. Have you found anything?"

"Some linens mostly. And a diary. I was just going to look at it when you came up." Jennie ran her hand over the cover. She wouldn't read it now, she decided. She'd wait until she had some time alone. Jennie started to put the book back and discovered a second diary in the drawer. She decided to take them with her to the castle and wrapped them in a linen tablecloth.

While Jennie was doing that, Shelagh went to a large trunk. "I've been wishing I could have a look in this. Look,

Jennie. It has a label on it from Paris. No one ever said anything about Mary being a traveler. I asked Grandie about it, but she had no idea. According to her, Mary never liked to travel except for one time when she stayed up in Galway and worked for Mrs. McDermott."

"Who's that?"

"I'm not certain. I think she ran an inn. Grandie says that's where Mary met Hugh. Said I'd have to wait until Helen opened it. Maybe Mary and Uncle Hugh went to Paris on their honeymoon. What do you suppose is in it?"

Jennie set the diaries on the dresser near the candle so she wouldn't forget them. "I have no clue. Go ahead and open it."

"Are you ready?" Shelagh's braces flashed in the scant light. She lifted the latch and started to pull up the lid but then stopped. "Do you suppose she'll mind?"

"Mary? She's dead."

"Aye, but her spirit lives on. And who knows what secrets are hidden here?"

"I think you're trying to scare me. It's just a trunk. If you don't want to open it, I will. It's not like something's going to jump out at you or anything." Jennie had heard enough talk about spirits and ghosts. This was her great-grandmother's trunk. And she wanted to see what was inside.

"I'll open it, but we mustn't hurry a moment like this. It's to be savored."

"You savor a good meal. You open trunks." Despite her brave words, Jennie held her breath as Shelagh eased open the heavy lid.

Nothing came flying out. No wind, no spirits. Still, with the opening of the trunk came a hush, an odd stillness as though it really were a special event—an almost reverent moment. Jennie could hardly take it in. She let out a breath in a swish and closed the lid. "I can't. Not yet." Jennie tried to put into words what she felt but couldn't. She had a better sense of what Gram must have meant by saying she wasn't ready. *Mary lived here. And died here.* Everything she possessed had either been carted up into the attic or given away. The enormity of life and death stretched over Jennie, making it hard to breathe.

"Why?"

Jennie's gaze moved from the trunk to her cousin's face.

"Are you all right, Jennie? You look as though you've seen a ghost."

"Not a ghost. It's just . . . I don't know. I feel like I'm intruding. Gram should be the one to open it. Not me." Jennie scrambled to her feet, nearly hitting her head on a rafter. "Besides, I thought we were going on a picnic."

"Oh." Shelagh bounced up. "I nearly forgot. Jeremy and Sean are likely waiting for us in the stables."

"Then let's go."

Shelagh took the candle and matches, and Jennie grabbed the linen-wrapped diaries.

Once downstairs, Jennie tucked the diaries into her backpack while Shelagh gathered the food and let the adults know where they were going. Minutes later Shelagh and Jennie jogged down to the road toward the castle. The stables were situated on the east side, near what Shelagh called the carriage house. It was actually a fancy garage with four deep stalls. Tucked into one was the car Declan had picked them up in. In another sat a convertible—an antique bright yellow Roadster with its hood up. A man stood next to it. He waved when he saw them.

Shelagh waved back, and Jennie did as well. "Who's that?"

"Mac."

"Megan's father?"

"Aye. He works on all the autos. Even ours when me da gets stumped."

"Neat car," Jennie said. "Whose is it?"

"William's."

They took the road around to the other side and came

to a large corral, where several horses grazed.

"We were just going out to find you." Sean and Jeremy were already mounted and leading two horses. "What took you so long?"

Jeremy smirked. "They're women, Sean. You know better than to ask. Women are always late."

"We are not late. It's just now four o'clock." Shelagh slapped at Jeremy's leg. "You are early."

Jeremy handed Shelagh the reins to her horse. "You came late on purpose so you wouldn't have to saddle up."

"You have us there, Jeremy," Jennie teased. "Thanks." Sean handed Jennie the reins to what was to be her mount. Turning back to Jeremy, she added, "Nice horse."

Jeremy's eyes gleamed with what Jennie thought was pride. He seemed happier, and Jennie wondered if he'd resolved things with his father.

"Her name's Ranie," he said. "She's one of William's favorite mares. She'll do well by you."

"Hello, Ranie." Jennie ran her hands down the mare's silken neck. Her shiny coat was the color of dark molasses. Jennie held an apple she'd taken from the table out for Ranie to nibble. Ranie nickered her thanks, chomped it down, and nuzzled Jennie for more. "I think they should have called you Miss Piggy." Jennie grabbed the saddle horn and placed her left foot in the saddle, preparing to mount. The saddle slid down around Ranie's belly, and in the next instant Jennie was on the ground. Her yelp sent the horses whinnying and prancing.

The boys howled with laughter. "Oh, look at that." Sean doubled over. "Must have forgotten to tighten it."

"Sean Keegan, this was your doing, wasn't it?" Shelagh scolded, offering Jennie a hand up. "Are you hurt?"

Jennie dusted herself off. "No, I'm fine."

"That was not funny," Shelagh yelled at the boys. "I suppose you forgot to tighten mine as well."

Jeremy dismounted and came to Shelagh's side. "Here, I'll do it for you." He was still laughing. "Jennie, you should have seen the look on your face."

"Priceless." Sean jumped down and reached for Ranie's saddle.

Jennie slapped his hand away. "I'll do it myself. See if I trust you two again."

By the time she'd properly saddled her horse and mounted, Jennie's sense of humor had returned. They'd had a good laugh at her expense, but she didn't mind. She would just look for an opportunity to pay them back.

With their picnic stashed in saddlebags, the foursome headed out. They took the path to the beach that Gram and Jennie had taken earlier, but instead of turning toward the farmhouse, they headed north. They hit the sand running and let the horses go full out once they reached the sand left firm by the outgoing tide. Their run was short-lived, as the mile-long stretch of beach turned rocky. As they approached the rocks, they turned inland, following a well-worn path up the rugged hillside and into the woods. When they slowed, the boys rode ahead. "You've done some riding, then, Jennie," Shelagh said. "You're handling Ranie well."

"Some. My aunt Maggie and uncle Jeff have a dude ranch in western Montana. I learned to ride there. I've done a little riding since then. Love it," she added.

"Except when certain people play tricks on you."

Jennie chuckled. "I gave them a good laugh, at least."

Shelagh's lips widened in a reluctant grin. "You're a good sport."

"Not always. I'm not much into practical jokes."

"Sometimes they serve a purpose, but Sean carries them too far. He's a terrible tease. Mum and Da get after him all the time, but it never stops him. Sometimes I do little things to get even." The mischievous look in her cousin's eyes told Jennie the games had just begun. She found herself enjoying the idea of a payback.

The path wound through the woods but never far from the ocean. Jennie could see the sun glistening on the water through the trees. The air was crisp and invigorating. If someone had asked her to describe paradise, she would come up with a scene like this.

A few minutes later they came out of the woods and onto a bluff situated high above the sea. The cliffs seemed to run straight up and down and go on for miles. They stopped at a place where the woods backed away and left a wide clearing. Emerald grasses and dainty flowers covered the ground.

"Is this where we'll have our picnic?" Jennie asked.

"It is." Shelagh dismounted and waited for Jennie to do the same. They brought their saddlebags to the spot where the boys were laying out a gray woolen blanket.

"What are we eating?" Jennie asked.

"We're having an American feast in your honor," Shelagh said.

"Hot dogs roasted on an open fire." Jeremy pulled a package of sausages out of a paper bag. "We'll have to get a fire going first. You and Shelagh can help us gather firewood."

Within a few minutes they had a fire and had spread out a feast of potato chips, carrot sticks, pickles, mustard, and buns. Jeremy and Sean poked sticks they'd whittled to fine points into two hot dogs and handed them to Jennie and Shelagh to roast before fixing their own.

Jennie placed her hot dog near the flame, watching the juices drip and the meat brown and plump.

"These smell wonderful," Shelagh said. " 'Tis a treat for us."

Sean and Jeremy found a spot in the fire for their hot dogs as well. The smug look on their faces gave Jennie an idea. She gazed intently at the dog Jeremy had handed her and, her suspicious mind being what it was, suspected foul play. "Did you put something in these hot dogs?" she asked. "Like a worm or something?"

Sean sniggered. "That's gross. Not even Jeremy or I would think of something like that."

Jeremy shook his head. "We have our standards. We'll not be tampering with good food."

"Yeah, I'll bet." No way did Jennie believe them. "Then you won't mind trading with us."

The boys looked at each other and shrugged. "Sure, why not?"

Jennie felt foolish when nothing came of her claim of foul play. But her mistake was soon forgotten. The meal was perfect. The boys ate three hot dogs each, Jennie and Shelagh only two. They snacked on chips and carrots.

At the end of the meal, Shelagh pulled out another sack. "Dessert!" The bag was full of chocolate chip cookies.

"When did you bake those?" Jennie asked.

"This morning before school," Shelagh answered.

Jennie should have guessed that her cousin was up to something when she so carefully doled out the cookies. Three for each of the guys first, then two each for herself and Jennie.

Jennie bit into the chewy cookie. Tender, not too sweet, and yummy chocolate. There was a spice or flavoring she wasn't familiar with. "Mmm. Shelagh, these are really good. What's in them—I mean, besides the usual?"

"That would be cardamom."

"Ieeyiii." Jeremy, who'd practically swallowed one cookie whole and was halfway into the second, yowled. His face turned lobster red. He spit out the cookie and held his throat.

Sean seemed to be in a similar fix. Jennie looked from the cookie she was eating to Shelagh, who was now laughing uncontrollably. Through giggles, chortles, and snorts, she managed to give an explanation. Shelagh had doctored Sean's and Jeremy's cookies with hot peppers and bitter chocolates.

"Shelagh, how cruel." Jennie tried to keep a straight face but couldn't. Jeremy and Sean guzzled down the rest of the water. Feeling sorry for them, Jennie took out the rest of the hot dog buns. "Try bread. It'll absorb the heat."

They did as she suggested.

Shelagh collapsed on the blanket, holding her stomach and moaning. "My stomach hurts," she gasped. "Haven't laughed so hard in ages." Tears rolled down her cheeks.

When the guys had recovered enough to talk, Sean turned on Shelagh. "I'll get you for that."

Shelagh screamed, rolled away from him, clambered to her feet, and raced toward the woods, then back.

Jeremy brushed tears from his face. "I may never eat another cookie as long as I live."

"I can't believe she did that." Jennie laughed at the two siblings racing around the picnic area. "I hope he doesn't hurt her."

Sean seemed angry enough to do serious damage if he did manage to catch Shelagh.

"Naw. They're always at each other. She'll be—" Jeremy gasped.

Jennie lurched forward as she saw the earth itself give way beneath Sean and Shelagh. Sean dove away from the cliff. Shelagh went down with a huge chunk of earth as it fell into the sea.

13

"Shelagh!" Sean wailed. Lying on the ground, he peered over the edge of the cliff. "Hold on."

"Help me!" Shelagh screamed. "I'm slipping."

He glanced back toward Jennie and Jeremy, who were already running toward him. "You've got to help me. She's just hanging there. I don't know how much longer she can hold on. Rocks are slippery."

"The ground's unstable, Sean," Jennie warned. "Come back away from the edge before you go down too."

The earth still hadn't stopped its downward fall. Most of the debris had fallen into the ocean some twenty feet below. Jennie leaned out over the precipice. Rocks and dirt and grass were still sliding into the churning water. Shelagh hung from a rock about four feet from the top of the cliff. Dirt clung to her hair and tear-streaked face.

"One of us should go for help." Jeremy stood next to Jennie, a hand on her shoulder.

"There's no time. She can't hold on much longer." Sean stretched forward until only his hips and legs remained on the ground, the rest of his body suspended over the edge.

"Sean, no!" Jennie yelled. "Wait. Jeremy, lie down behind him and grab his legs. I have an idea." She yanked up the blanket, sending their picnic items flying. Hurrying back to the cliff, she gave Sean one end of the blanket and tossed the other over the edge. "Shelagh, hold on to the blanket. We'll pull you up. Sean, scoot back so you don't fall down too." Sean started to argue but then did as Jennie asked.

"I can't," Shelagh cried.

"You have to," Jennie called. "Just hold tight." The three of them coaxed and encouraged Shelagh, drawing her upward until Sean was able to take hold of her arms and pull her the rest of the way to safety.

"Do you have a first-aid kit?" Jennie, using methods she'd learned in her first-aid classes, examined Shelagh for injuries.

"There's one in my saddlebags," Jeremy answered. "Dad won't let me ride without one."

"What are you doing?" Sean asked. "You're acting like a doctor or something."

Jennie told them about the first-aid training she'd had. "Comes in handy."

"So what's the diagnosis?" Jeremy knelt beside her, setting the white box between them.

A smile tugged at Jennie's mouth. No one had ever asked her that before. A fleeting image flashed through her mind. She imagined herself in scrubs, examining a patient in the emergency room. *Dr. Jennifer McGrady.*

Has a nice ring to it.

Jennie dismissed the fantasy. *You're going into law enforcement, not medicine, remember?*

Using water from their canteens, Jennie cleaned up the worst of Shelagh's scrapes and cuts, applying bandages to two of them.

Moments later, they all lay on the damp, cool ground, exhausted from the ordeal.

"How can I ever thank you?" Shelagh said. "You saved my life. Especially you, Jennie. You were so calm and knew just what to do."

Jennie didn't feel calm. At the moment her knees felt like Jell-O on a warm day.

Sean rolled over on his stomach and got to his knees.

"You've only yourself to blame, Shelagh Marie Keegan. Feeding us those cookies. The only reason I saved you was so I could get back at you."

"I don't believe you two." Jennie turned to Jeremy. "Are they always like this?"

"Actually, since they've got company, they're on their best behavior." Having gotten to his feet, he reached toward Jennie to give her a hand up.

"I'm cold." Shelagh still sat on the ground and had begun to shake.

Jennie snagged the blanket and wrapped it around her. "Are you sure you're all right? Do you hurt anywhere?"

"I'm f-fine." Her mouth quivered. "Just feeling a bit shaky and weak."

"No wonder, after what you've been through."

"We'd best be getting back," Sean said after they'd rested. "It's nearly seven. It will be dark soon."

They gathered all of their picnic supplies and leftover food, doused the fire, and headed out. Jennie rode near Shelagh so she could watch her, though it probably wasn't necessary. About halfway into the ride, Shelagh seemed to have recovered completely and had returned to being her animated self.

They took a different route back. Jeremy and Sean said it would be faster. They went inland more—through the woods and over pastureland, finally ending up on a paved road. The road was the same one Declan had taken when Jennie and Gram arrived the day before. Jennie recognized Saint Matthew's Church and the graveyard where she and Gram had stopped.

As they came upon the cemetery, the sun had disappeared into the rising mist. The crosses and statues loomed black against the darkening gray sky. A chilling wind was blowing in from the north, making it feel more like February than May.

" 'Tis a scary place at night," Shelagh said in a quivery voice.

Jennie had to admit it was. "Have you ever been in it at night?"

"Once. Sean thought it would be fun to spend the night here." Shelagh expelled a nervous giggle. "We were home before midnight."

"What happened?"

"The door to one of the tombs opened."

Sean spread his arms. "And this huge monster came out."

"Give me a break. Do you expect me to believe that?"

"It's true. Isn't it, Shelagh. Saw it with our own eyes."

" 'Tis true, Jennie."

"You're saying there's a monster in the cemetery?" Jeremy scoffed at the idea.

"We are."

"Shelagh." Sean slowed his horse. "It does no good to tell Americans anything. They don't have the Irish way of believing."

"I think a lot depends on what we're supposed to believe," Jeremy said.

"The mysteries." Sean stopped at the cemetery gate. "Leprechauns, ghosts, monsters. Even God himself."

"Humph." Jeremy scowled. "Maybe you're right. I don't believe in much. Sometimes I don't even believe in what I do see."

"I believe in God," Jennie said. "And I believe in miracles. But if you saw or think you saw a monster, there's an explanation for it. It was probably just a big person or the shadow of a tree moving in the wind." Jennie knew firsthand the kinds of tricks the imagination could play on someone. "I'll bet it was the gardener. I saw him yesterday when we came here. He's pretty big."

" 'Twasn't." Sean guided his horse along the stone wall around the cemetery. When he reached the end, he lifted his leg over the saddle horn and pivoted in his saddle, scooted over to the wall, and jumped to the other side.

"What are you doing, Sean?" Shelagh whispered. "We need to be getting home."

"I'm going to prove I'm right. Come on."

"This isn't a good idea." Jennie frowned.

"It's all right, Jennie." Shelagh followed Sean's lead. "We probably won't see the monster. If we do, he likely won't hurt us. We can run faster, that's certain."

Jeremy clambered over the fence after Shelagh, leaving Jennie alone with the horses.

"Come on, Jennie," Shelagh urged. "You won't be wanting to stay here by yourself."

"Yes, I will. You guys go ahead." Jennie waited several minutes, listening for their voices. Soon the whispers stopped, and Jennie heard nothing but branches swishing and clicking in the wind. After what had to be ten minutes of silence, Jennie thought she heard a muffled groan.

"Jennie," Shelagh whispered. "Come quick. Jeremy's been hurt."

"Serves him right, wandering around out here in the dark. What happened?"

"He's tripped on something. Sean's not strong enough to carry him."

"Can't you help him?"

"I'm not strong enough. Besides, you've had first-aid training. Sean said you'll know what to do."

Jennie took a deep breath, slipped from her saddle onto the wall, and jumped down. The wall was only about four feet tall, shorter than she'd originally thought.

"Come on." Shelagh took hold of Jennie's hand and dragged her through the rows of graves.

"Where is he?"

"Back here. Hurry. We have to get out of here before the monster comes."

Jennie didn't know whether to be afraid or angry. She was a whole lot of both at the moment. She paused when they came across the Celtic cross atop Mary O'Donnell's grave. The cross was a symbol of eternal life, reminding

Jennie she had nothing to fear. The spirit of God was stronger than anything she might encounter, imagined or otherwise. Jennie felt the tug of Shelagh's hand and heard another groan. This was no time to be thinking of fear. Jeremy was hurt.

Shelagh let out a gasp and stopped so suddenly that Jennie nearly ran into her. "What's wrong?" she whispered.

"They were here, Jennie. Right here. Something's happened. Maybe the monster's come after them."

"Shelagh, don't be silly." Jennie swallowed back her own fear as she saw that the door to one of the tombs stood open, revealing a dark, yawning cavern.

"Sean?" Shelagh called in a hoarse whisper. "Jeremy?"

"I'll bet they're inside." Jennie turned back to Shelagh, but she was gone.

Jennie shrugged and turned back to the open tomb and stepped inside—sure that she'd find the boys hiding and waiting to jump out. She wished she had a flashlight. The outside light was practically gone. Jennie ventured another step inside. The tomb smelled earthy, musty. She heard a scuffling noise outside and froze.

The shadowy light left by the remnants of sunset disappeared as the door slammed shut behind her.

Jennie gasped for breath and finally found it. She felt her way to where the door should have been. "Jeremy! Sean! Let me out this minute. Shelagh!"

Jennie ran her hand over metal and wood. No handle. She sat back against the wall, not wanting to believe her cousins could have tricked her again—or that she could have fallen for it. Though she couldn't hear them, she suspected they and Jeremy were howling over their stupid prank.

"I've had it," she mumbled. "When I get my hands on you, I'll . . ." *You'll what? Hit them? Pull some kind of prank on them to get even?* It was all a silly game, and the mature thing to do would be to ignore them. Pretty hard to do when they insisted on graveyard visitations and pushing her into an open tomb. She frowned. Why had it been open, anyway? Had they opened it and then lured her in? How long did they intend to leave her there? Surely not all night. Would they?

"Sean, Shelagh! I'm really tired of this," she yelled.

No response.

She banged on the door. "Let me out."

Still no response.

"Come on, you guys. I mean it."

They weren't going to listen. Maybe they'd already gone home. Fine. She'd like to hear them explain to Gram and their parents what they did to their cousin. Jennie lowered herself to what felt like a concrete floor and pulled her knees up, wrapping her arms around them. All she wanted to do was go back to the castle, take a long hot bath, and go to bed. She hated the dark. She listened intently for voices but heard nothing. Silent as a tomb. If she hadn't been so tired and angry, she might have laughed at the thought.

Jennie thought about getting up and feeling her way around the place, but she couldn't make herself move. She didn't know anything about tombs other than that they were burial places. Chances are she was sharing her space with a dead body. Space that had no air. Dead bodies didn't need oxygen. Had her cousins and Jeremy thought about that? "If I die in here, the joke will be on you, won't it," she mumbled.

Don't think about dying. Focus on something pleasant. Your cousins aren't going to let you die. At the worst, they'll probably leave you here all night.

She couldn't imagine Shelagh doing that. Jennie hugged her legs tighter. It was cold but not unbearable. Thankfully, Jennie had worn a warm sweater and had a wool scarf around her neck.

Pleasant thoughts, she reminded herself. *Think about good things.* Not easy when you were sitting in a tomb. She closed her eyes and imagined herself sitting on the rocks near her grandmother's home on the Oregon coast. With Ryan. In a way it pleased her to think she might be spending time with him again. Then again, she was still upset with him for dumping her.

Jennie focused on taking slow, even breaths and thinking about walking on the beach and going to the coast aquarium in Newport, Oregon, and watching the white lacy jellyfish dancing in their big glass tube.

She rested her head on her arms and at some point drifted off to sleep.

———

"Jennie." A voice drifted down a long chamber. She was lying on satin. Arms at her side. In a box. It had a lid. A coffin. Her eyes were closed and she couldn't open them, but she could see. She could feel her arms and legs, but they were heavy and she couldn't move them.

"Jennie." Someone was calling her. Gram.

Jennie tried to answer but couldn't. The lid began to close.

"No!" She screamed for them to stop. No sound came out of her mouth. The lid fell with a thud. Dead. They thought she was dead.

Then, instead of darkness there was light . . . bright moving light.

"Jennie." Someone slid an arm under her shoulders and lifted her up.

"Is she all right?" Shelagh asked.

Jennie opened her eyes, and the nightmare vanished. "No thanks to you," she muttered as she gave her cousin a withering look.

Thomas helped her into a sitting position. "Shelagh, what's she saying? Have you and Sean been up to your old tricks again?"

"No, Da. We didn't do this." Shelagh looked genuinely surprised. "Jennie, we truly didn't."

"Oh please, Shelagh. You led me in here. You said Jeremy had been hurt. And the next thing I knew, I was locked in a tomb."

"He was hurt. Honestly. I'd not lie to you. I saw him fall myself. He's at the castle right now with ice on his foot."

"Well, if you didn't lock me in, who did? We were the only ones in the cemetery."

"Girls, girls," Gram interrupted. "We can straighten this out later. Right now we need to get you back to the castle. Jennie, can you walk, or do you need Thomas to carry you?"

"I can walk." Jennie held on to Thomas's arm for balance. "What time is it?"

"Ten-thirty."

She'd been entombed for over three hours. Gram's flashlight filled the small square area with light—enough to see that there was no body. Roughhewn boards made shelves along the back wall. Garden tools of all sorts hung on hooks along another wall. At the far end was a wheelbarrow and shovel.

Everything was neatly placed. Jennie frowned. "This isn't a tomb?"

"It's the gardener's shed." Father O'Roarke appeared behind Gram. "It was once meant to be a tomb but was never used. It seemed the ideal place to store the gardening tools and such."

"But I couldn't get out."

"There's a latch outside. We keep it locked—things have a habit of wandering off when we don't."

"Ah, you've found her, then." William and Sean came into view. "How did you get to be in the tool shed?"

"Ask Sean and Shelagh," Jennie grumped. "They locked me in."

"Don't you worry, Jennie," Thomas grumbled. "If my two are responsible for this, they'll suffer great consequences."

Jennie bit her lip, wishing now she hadn't said anything. It had been a prank. She'd fallen for it. "It's okay," she said. "I wasn't hurt or anything."

"But we didn't do it, Da," Shelagh insisted. "It must have been the monster."

Jennie groaned. "Can't you come up with something better than that?"

"We'll talk about it when we get home." Thomas tightened his grip on Jennie when she stumbled over a rock.

Gram's flashlight beam mingled with Father O'Roarke's as they trooped through the cemetery and back to the gate, which now stood open. William's yellow Roadster and Thomas's car were parked just outside.

"I'll take Helen and Jennie back to the castle," William offered. "I suspect they'll both be wanting to wash up and get to bed soon."

William helped Jennie into the backseat. Sean and Shelagh stood at the side of the car, both apparently wanting to say something. Jennie moved her unforgiving gaze from one to the other.

"We weren't the only ones in the cemetery, Jennie." Shelagh grasped the top of the back door. "Declan was here. He's the one who found us and took Jeremy home. He helped us look for you for a bit and then told us you likely had gone home."

"The monster must have locked you in there." Sean glanced back in the direction of the old tomb. "There's no other explanation."

"We both know there was no monster." Jennie leaned back against the seat. "It's no big deal, okay? You got me. Just admit you did it and let's be done with it."

"But I didn't," Shelagh said again. "I went round to where Sean and Jeremy were, and then we came back to find you but you were gone."

Shelagh looked miserable, and Jennie began having doubts about her guilt. Still, Shelagh had been with her. She'd been leading Jennie to Jeremy and Sean. At the tomb Jennie remembered looking around and discovering Shelagh wasn't there. Maybe she was innocent. But she doubted very much if she could say the same about Sean.

They arrived at the castle around eleven o'clock. Jennie showered, slipped into her pajamas, and tapped on Gram's door.

"Come in." Gram was already in bed, reading. She patted the covers beside her. "You're welcome to sleep with me tonight if you'd like."

Jennie gave her a hug and nodded. "Thanks. I was hoping you'd ask. This place is giving me the creeps."

Gram set her book on the nightstand, snapped off the light, and snuggled down under the covers. "I'm afraid your first taste of Ireland hasn't been very pleasant."

"Parts of it, anyway. We had a nice visit with Bridget and Catherine. And the horse ride and picnic were great until . . ." Jennie told Gram about the loose saddles and Shelagh's cookies and about almost losing Shelagh when the cliff gave way.

"I'm glad she's safe. I'd forgotten what teases those children can be. I should have warned you." Gram chuckled. "Shelagh really put peppers and bitter chocolate in her cookies?"

"Yeah."

"I'll have to remember that. Interesting way to get revenge."

Jennie made a face. "I'm just glad she didn't give me one." She turned onto her side and propped her elbow on the bed, holding her head in her hand. "She didn't give me one."

"So you said."

"No, I mean Shelagh wouldn't have locked me in that tomb in the cemetery. She wasn't trying to get back at me."

"No, but children always seem fascinated by graves and such. They may have been planning it all along."

Jennie sighed. "They told me they'd seen a monster in

the cemetery and were going to prove it to me."

"And you believed them?"

"No. But I don't think Shelagh was making it up. She must have seen something—or someone."

"The gardener, perhaps. Or Father O'Roarke. Both are large men, and in the dark Shelagh and Sean may have imagined they were monsters."

"Shelagh said Declan had been there tonight." Jennie frowned. "You don't suppose he . . ."

"Of course not. Declan saw the horses at the cemetery on his way home. Since it was getting dark and you children had no business there, he stopped. It was then he discovered Jeremy had twisted his ankle. He helped them look for you and then took Jeremy home."

"Find me, humph. Like they didn't know where I was."

"According to the version I heard, they looked around but couldn't find you. They thought maybe you'd gotten upset or frightened and walked home."

"Why would I do that? I wouldn't have left the horses."

"Well, I can understand their thinking. You weren't in the cemetery—that they could see, anyway."

"How come it took so long to find me?"

"Sean and Shelagh were so sure you'd walked back to the castle. It seemed the natural thing to do. Seeing the state Shelagh was in, I felt certain you'd want to clean up before coming back to the farmhouse. I wasn't worried at that point. When I went back to the castle and discovered you weren't there, I called out the guards. William and Thomas drove along the roads and walked back along the path. Since the last place they'd seen you was in the cemetery, we went back there for another look around. Shelagh showed me where you'd disappeared. I saw the locked door and, well, call it intuition. I had a strong hunch you were inside. Father O'Roarke, who was helping us by then, unlocked it, and there you were."

Jennie barely heard the last few words and was vaguely

aware of Gram's hand brushing back her hair and kissing her cheek. "Good night, sweetheart."

"Night." Jennie nuzzled her face into the pillow.

There were no ghostly wanderings that night, no groans, no wind opening windows or rain slashing against the panes. Or if there were, Jennie didn't hear them.

14

Jennie wakened to the gentle strains of an Irish lullaby. Gram was singing in the shower again.

Jennie stretched and yawned, debating whether or not to get up. Gram had opened the blinds to the patio doors, giving Jennie a wonderful view of the ocean without her having to move. Seeing the water took her back to the day before. How close they'd come to losing Shelagh. Jennie wasn't angry anymore about being locked in the gardening shed. She hadn't even been that frightened. Well, maybe a little. It seemed like a bad dream now—one she didn't want to repeat.

Gram came in, wrapped in a white terry robe and a pink towel around her head. "Hey, you're awake."

"No thanks to you," Jennie teased. "Do you always sing in the shower?"

"No. Only when I'm in Ireland—in a castle. Something about waking up to that spectacular view just makes me want to sing."

Jennie yawned again as she slid up to sit against the headboard. "It is nice."

"Do you have any plans for the day?"

"Nope." Jennie rubbed a tender spot on her neck. It was probably the result of falling asleep on the concrete floor of the gardening shed. "Do you?"

"Hmm. William asked if I wanted to spend the day

looking into Liam's death. I'll go to the library and possibly to the monastery."

"The monastery?"

"Yes. They'd have a record of his death, and there may be some notes from the priest at that time. If there's time, we can talk to some old-timers who might remember Liam and be able to shed some light on his death."

"Oh. So it sounds as though you have your whole day planned." Jennie tried not to look disappointed. Though she didn't have plans of her own, she wasn't too excited about spending the day alone while Gram was out working on a murder case.

Gram must have noticed her reticence. "You're welcome to come along with us."

"I'd like that."

"I'll tell William you're coming."

Half an hour later they joined William in the dining room for breakfast. Jeremy and Declan had eaten and gone. Not surprising, since it was already nine-thirty.

"Good morning." An elderly woman with a husky voice and flaming red hair came into the room. Her long, velvety green dress swayed as she walked.

"Mother." William bounced up and hurried to her side. He offered her an arm. She slipped her left hand through it and, using the cane in her right hand, shuffled to the table, where William pulled out a chair. "I didn't know you were coming down. You should have called for help."

"Nonsense. I'm perfectly capable of walking." To Jennie and Gram she said, "Thinks I'm an invalid."

"Mother, this is—"

"I know perfectly well who my guests are. Be a good boy and tell Megan I want some tea."

When he'd gone, she leaned forward and in a conspiratorial voice said, "I'm Maude Kavanagh," for Jennie's benefit. "Now, Helen, you must tell me how your visit is going. Have you seen Catherine? Poor dear was so looking forward to your visit. Is she doing any better?"

William returned before Gram could answer, and behind him came Megan with Maude's tea.

"I was just asking about Catherine, William."

"She's doing well," Gram said. "Of course, they're all rather upset about the fire."

"Yes, I heard. How dreadful. Declan seems to think it was set on purpose."

"Looks that way."

"What's the world coming to? There are hooligans everywhere. Even in our area." Maude poured tea from the pot into a gold-rimmed teacup. "And how about you, Jennie? Are you enjoying your stay? Jeremy told me about your picnic." Her eyebrows raised. "Apparently the Keegan children are still up to their old tricks. And you poor dear, being shut up in that old tomb. Must have been terrifying."

"A little. How is Jeremy's ankle?"

"He was still hobbling around on it this morning." The duchess paused to take a sip of tea. "Declan's taken him to the doctor to have it X-rayed. I suspect they'll fit him with crutches and send him on his way. Serves the boy right, prowling around cemeteries. Children these days have no respect for the dead."

"Oh, now, I'm sure that's not true. They were just having a bit of harmless fun," William said.

"Humph. Now, Helen," Maude said, abruptly changing the subject, "you must tell me all about your family."

Gram did, and the duchess listened. Jennie found the older woman fascinating and couldn't seem to stop looking at her. She was obviously wearing a wig. She also wore makeup—lots of it—yet didn't seem overly done. She had soft features and more weight than was probably healthy.

"Declan and William told us about your move here from England," Jennie said during a lull in the conversation. "That must have been quite the adventure."

"I've my father to thank for it. At first I was furious

that he'd marry me off to some Celtic savage. Even if he was from the ruling class, I wanted nothing to do with the Irish. The English thought them absurdly stupid, you know." She glanced at Helen and William. "Of course, they proved me wrong, but for years we couldn't understand how the Irish could have gotten themselves into that famine business. They were surrounded by the sea. They could have brought in food from other countries." The duchess waved her hand. "But that's history, isn't it. I fought coming here at first. But my father insisted. My journey to Ireland was frightening for a young girl. I was only sixteen, mind you. Your age, Jennie, isn't it?"

Jennie nodded. "I can't imagine my father sending me to some other country to marry someone. He barely lets me out of the house to go out with my friends."

"Yes, things have certainly changed, haven't they?"

Jennie frowned. "So you were only twenty or so when Liam died."

"Yes, and with a three-year-old," Gram said. "That must have been terribly difficult for you."

"Not so bad. Liam was not a very attentive husband. Once we married I hardly ever saw him. I think he was afflicted with some kind of illness, but he never said. Oh, not that he neglected his duties. He provided well for William and me."

"William asked me to look into Liam's death. Has he talked with you about it?" Gram set her spoon down and lifted her cup to her lips. Jennie perked up at Gram's question. She listened intently for any clue the duchess might be able to provide.

"William has the foolish notion his father was murdered. I've tried to talk him out of it. Does no good at all to dig into past events." Maude sighed. "I prefer to dwell on the good memories."

She patted her son's hand. "All your questions will come to no good, I'm afraid. I'm tired, William. See me to my room." To Gram and Jennie she said, "I do hope you'll forgive me. I seem to tire easily these days. I'll see you at dinner?"

"Yes." Gram stood when the duchess did.

William excused himself and offered his mother his arm. She leaned heavily on him as she walked, her limp more pronounced.

Gram smiled. "All this time and she's still the proper British lady."

―――――――――

Deciding to spend the day with Gram and William had been a mistake, Jennie realized as they stopped at a pub for a lunch of fish and chips. They were trying to find some of Liam's acquaintances, and they had. But so far the ones they'd spoken to contributed nothing new. Their stories were embellished, and Jennie doubted any of them were true. Several admitted that they, too, had questioned the idea that Liam could have fallen. One, a retired police officer, had agreed to have lunch with them while they chatted. He'd been called out to the castle to investigate the accident.

" 'Twas a baffling case," the officer said. "No evidence of foul play. Well, not a case, really. I thought all the while it must have been a suicide. The duchess would have none of that kind of talk. According to her there was nothing in his life terrible enough to make him want to kill himself."

"What did you finally decide?" Gram asked.

"We didn't. We could never prove anything one way or the other. A true mystery, it was. Family man. Handsome wife, young son. He had everything to live for. And he was a kindly man, always giving to this cause and that. No one seemed to carry a grudge. He had no enemies that we could find and more than his share of friends."

"What was your take on it?" Gram asked. "Surely you had an opinion."

"An accident, more than likely. Perhaps he took it into his head to lean over the wall. Might have done so if he'd seen something amiss—a piece of trash or something."

So far this man was the only person who'd come up with a viable story. Most of the people felt certain Liam had angered one of the castle ghosts. But if he was such a nice guy, that didn't make any sense at all.

"Had he been drinking?" Gram split open a steaming piece of deep-fried fish.

The retired officer frowned. "As I recall, Liam wasn't a drinking man. Not in public, at least. But now that you mention it, there had been the smell of liquor, which would have accounted for his being careless. May have gotten it into his head to balance atop the wall."

They speculated a little more over the remains of their lunch, and before long Jennie, Gram, and William went back to the car.

Jennie wondered how much of the testimonies they heard could be trusted. The men were all in their seventies and eighties. Jennie began to wonder if they'd be able to solve the old mystery. Had too much time passed, after all?

"You're awfully quiet, Jennie." Gram turned around in her seat. "Are you all right?"

"Just tired." Jennie leaned forward. "Do you have more people to talk to?"

"Not today. We thought we'd head over to the monastery and look through some records." William backed out into the road.

"If you're bored, we can take you back to the castle," Gram said.

"No. That's okay."

While Gram and William pursued obituaries and newspaper articles, Jennie discovered the department where birth, death, and marriage records were kept.

"I have to do a genealogy report for school," Jennie told the library attendant.

"We have a lot of guests who come here just for that

reason." The attendant was a young man wearing a robe like the kind used by monks for centuries. He introduced himself as Brother Andrew. "Tell me your last name and I'll help you get started."

"McGrady," she said. "My grandfather was Ian McGrady. He was born in County Cork. He married Helen O'Donnell."

"Ah . . . that shouldn't be hard to find." Andrew typed the information into the computer program and within seconds found a perfect match.

"Wow. It did all the work for me," Jennie remarked. "I thought I'd have to fill it all in myself." Ian McGrady's family tree went clear back to the sixteenth century. Along with it was a history of the clan and a coat of arms.

The attendant printed it out for Jennie and moved out of the seat. "Would you like to do one for your grandmother's side?"

"Sure." Jennie went back and found the new form and typed in her grandmother's name and age, along with the town.

The genealogical information appeared just as quickly: Mary and Hugh O'Donnell, Mary's parents, and her siblings. "This is so cool."

"We used to have to do all of these by hand. Computers are wonderful tools."

Jennie stared at the screen. "I think there's a mistake here, though."

"What's that?"

"My grandmother was born in 1943. It says here that Mary and Hugh were married only six months before she was born. There's an extra little line here—like maybe something is missing."

"There's a way to check." Andrew typed in Hugh O'Donnell's name and accessed his records. The marriage date was the same.

"It isn't unusual," Andrew said. "Oftentimes children were born 'early.' Of course, they were usually conceived out of wedlock. The parents didn't actually fool anyone. Fornication is perhaps the most common of sins."

Jennie frowned at the screen. She didn't like to think of her great-grandmother as having had sex before marriage. Maybe it shouldn't have mattered, but it did. "Um. Thanks for your help. I think I can work it okay now by myself."

"Certainly. If you need help, let me know."

Jennie printed out the forms for Hugh and Mary, still wondering if it had been a mistake. Maybe she'd show Gram and ask her about it. Or maybe she'd find an answer in Mary's diaries—which she hadn't had a chance to look at yet.

With Gram and William still head-to-head in front of a microfiche machine, Jennie looked up William's name and printed out the Kavanagh family history. She found herself going back generations and generations to actual royalty. The Kavanaghs *had* ruled Ireland.

From genealogies, Jennie went into Irish history. She spent the next hour reading about the battles and the famous potato famine. Maude's comments earlier had struck Jennie as unsympathetic. Yet she found herself wondering why so much tragedy had permeated the country. Why had so many perished of starvation when others survived?

Gram came up behind Jennie and massaged her shoulders. "Find anything interesting?"

"Yeah. I got our genealogy charts and some family history. There's something I wanted to ask you about." Jennie glanced at William and realized Gram might not want to talk about the family secret—if it was a family secret—in front of him. "I'll show you later. Did you find what you wanted?"

"Nothing new, I'm afraid. The inspector was right about the investigation never closing. It was labeled an accident that didn't rule out suicide. I'm afraid we've hit a dead end."

"Maybe something will turn up when we look through my father's belongings," William said. "My mother saved his writings and log books. I've perused a few things, but . . ." He brightened. "Perhaps you and I can go through them together, Helen."

"We'll save those for another day." Gram smiled up at him.

"I've invited your grandmother to take in a bit of golfing this afternoon at the country club on the south coast. Would ye like to join us, then, Jennie? We'd love to have you."

"I don't think so. I'm not much of a golfer. Now, if it were swimming . . . "

" 'Tis a county club. You're more than welcome to swim while we golf."

"Great." Jennie's mood brightened. She hadn't been swimming since before leaving home, and it was the one sport she loved doing most. Besides, going with Gram and William would provide a perfect excuse not to spend time with her cousins. After what happened the night before, Jennie wasn't ready to hang out with them.

Jennie gathered her papers and stuffed them into her backpack, which she'd retrieved from the Keegan place on their way out that morning. Mary's linen tablecloth and diaries were still inside. Since they had to stop at the castle for Jennie to get her swimsuit, she removed her genealogies and Mary's diaries from the backpack and put them in the drawer of the nightstand. She hesitated a long moment, thinking she should stay there and read through Mary's diaries but decided there would be plenty of time for that in the days ahead.

Trading her backpack for her beach bag, Jennie hurried back to the car, where Gram and William were waiting.

Swimming refreshed Jennie as it always did and put her

in a great mood. She was even agreeable to spending some time at the house with Shelagh and Sean. Her anger with them had dissipated, and now she looked forward to putting things straight and finding out what had actually happened at the cemetery.

They arrived back at the castle to find an invitation from the Keegans to join them for a Friday night celebration of Bridget's birthday at the local pub.

Jennie donned what she'd come to call her standard uniform: jeans and a sweater. This sweater was knitted in intricate cable designs, with a lavender Aran yarn that had come straight from the Aran Isles. Or so the saleswoman at the shop had told her. They'd stopped in town on the way back from the country club, and Jennie decided to buy the sweater she'd seen the day they arrived. She loved the feel of the soft wool.

————

They had a light dinner of salad and shrimp at the castle. Jeremy declined to go to the party, saying his ankle was swollen and painful. Jennie caught him as he was heading back to his room and asked him if he really had hurt his ankle or if it was part of their game.

"Sean and I were planning to scare you," he admitted, "but when you didn't come along in, we got tired of waiting and were going back out when I tripped on one of the marble slabs. I really did hurt my ankle."

"I'd like to know who locked me in that tomb."

"It wasn't me."

"Sean said he was with you the whole time. Is that true?"

"Most of the time. We heard you coming, and he went to get you. Then he came back, said someone else was out there."

Jennie frowned. "Your father. And that monster of Sean's."

Jeremy raised an eyebrow. "You don't think Dad . . ."

"Of course not. I think Sean did it. He looked sheepish when Gram found me."

"You're wrong about that."

"How can you be so sure?"

"Jennie, I know Sean. If he had locked you in that tomb, he'd have been bragging about it today. But he didn't say anything. He was upset when I asked. You're not still mad about it, are you?"

"No, just curious."

"Well, I guess I would be too."

"I wish you could come along."

"Nah. They'll spend the night dancing and singing. And they'll try their best to teach you how even if you don't want to."

Jennie chuckled. "They did that the night we had dinner here."

"It'll be worse, trust me. Besides, my ankle is still pretty sore."

"Why don't you like it here?" Jennie asked. "Ireland is beautiful, and people seem to really enjoy themselves. Your grandfather seems very nice."

"He is. I have all I could possibly want—except my friends back home . . . and my mother."

"Jennie," Gram called. "Are you ready?"

"Coming." Jennie turned back to Jeremy. "Sure you don't want to change your mind?"

"Positive. Have a good time."

"I will." Jennie chuckled. "As long as my cousins don't decide to pull another prank."

They reached Mulhaney's Pub around eight, and people were already singing and dancing. Shelagh and her mother were singing an Irish ballad, and Thomas was playing for them. Two other fiddlers accompanied them. Father O'Roarke was there as well, nodding his head to the music. Jeremy had been right. Even with Jennie's insistence that she had two left feet, her family, Gram included, got her to do some Irish clogging. She managed to move her feet without tripping over them and eventually came to enjoy it. Gram threatened to give her lessons when they got back to Portland. Jennie lasted about thirty minutes. Thirsty, and her legs feeling like wilted lettuce, she went back to the table. "You're not quitting already, are you, darling?"

Gram had been talking to William and stopped when Jennie approached.

"Just resting." Jennie sat down and poured herself a glass of water from the pitcher on the table.

William stood. "I'll see you tomorrow, then."

"Are you sure you don't want me to go along?"

"Wouldn't want to take you away from the celebration. At least not until you've had some cake. No, I may even be back."

He ambled outside.

"Where's he going?" Jennie asked.

"Home. Apparently the duchess isn't feeling well."

"That's too bad."

Gram nodded. "Hope it's nothing serious."

———

By ten, Jennie was ready to go home. She was hot and, after ordering a root beer, went outside for a few minutes. The lights were on in the shop windows, so Jennie wandered down the street. On her way back, she saw a bent-over figure setting something down near the door of the pub. At first Jennie thought it might be someone littering—a street person getting rid of a bottle in a brown bag. Jennie hadn't planned on picking up the bag or even looking at it, but as she approached the door, she heard a ticking noise. The hairs on her arms stood up like armed guards. A chill trickled down her spine. A bomb?

15

Jennie had heard about the unrest in Northern Ireland but didn't think the fighting extended this far. Still, without hesitation, she went back inside the pub and took Gram aside, telling her what she'd seen. Gram talked to Mr. Mulhaney, the owner. While he placed a call to the authorities, Gram and Thomas managed to begin an orderly exodus out the back door. They weren't taking any chances. Jennie was following Shelagh outside when the explosion hit. The force of it threw Jennie against her cousin and onto the grass behind the building. Jennie scrambled to her feet and got Shelagh up, urging her to run. The back of the building remained intact. It took several seconds before Jennie realized that Gram and Thomas and the owner were still inside.

The shattering noise gave way to a rain of glass and debris. Jennie ran back to the door and peered inside. "Gram?" she yelled. "Thomas!" Dust rained down on her, making it hard to breathe.

"Da!" Shelagh screamed and pushed around Jennie.

"Wait." One of the men outside tried to stop the girls from going in. "Can't have you going in there, lasses. Not safe." Jennie leaned around him and scanned the room but saw no sign of her grandmother.

Jennie offered a prayer as she stood there, her feet refusing to move. *Gram, where are you?* Had she gone out the front in search of the horrible man who'd done this?

Or was she caught under the rubble somewhere?

"But me da. He's hurt," Shelagh pleaded. "I need to see him."

Sean came up behind them. "Da's in there?"

Shelagh nodded and collapsed against him.

"Please." Jennie tried to push the man's arm away. "I've had first-aid training. Let me go in."

"All right, but I'll be going first. Everyone else back off, now. Come on, then. Let's see what we can do to help."

Thomas was on his knees by the time they reached him. His hair was dusted with plaster and debris. He seemed okay. With the other man's help, Thomas got to his feet, and they carefully made their way around the wreckage. Jennie looked for Gram again but didn't see her. Plaster dust still hung in the air in thick, suffocating clouds.

"Gram! Where are you?" Jennie called between coughs as she moved through the building.

The police arrived then with the emergency response team and led Jennie outside to where the others waited. "My grandmother," Jennie said. "She was still in there when the bomb went off."

"I'm sorry, miss. We'll find her. Stay out here where you'll be safe. The building will be unstable."

Another officer approached them. "You must be Jennie McGrady."

She blinked at him. How would he know her name? "Yes. What—" She grabbed his arm. "Did you find my grandmother?"

He frowned. "I'm sorry, no. I was told you found the bomb."

"Oh. Um, yes." Jennie explained how she'd gone outside and spotted the slumped-over man with the brown coat setting down the sack. "At first I thought he was a drunk getting rid of an empty bottle. Then when I went inside, I heard the ticking." Jennie glanced back inside. "I can't believe it was a real bomb. Who would do something like this? We were just having a birthday party."

"That's what we're intending to find out."

Jennie went back to where an EMT was trying to talk Thomas into going to the hospital.

He refused, saying he'd had nothing more than a bump on the head. "Just let me go home."

Bridget didn't agree. "You'll do no such thing, Thomas Keegan. If these men think you should see the doctor, you will—even if I have to drag you there myself."

Thomas gave in and went along in the ambulance, but only when he'd fainted dead away.

Shelagh came up to Jennie and wrapped her arms around Jennie's waist. "I hope they find your Gram soon, Jennie."

Jennie hugged Shelagh back, the warmth of it releasing the tears she'd refused to shed. "It seems so unreal." Jennie glanced around. "Catherine . . . is she. . . ?"

"She's fine. Da took her out first. She's sitting in the car."

Jennie shivered. The night air had a frosty feel to it again. *First the fire two nights ago. Tonight a bombing. What next?*

"She must be frightened out of her wits," Jennie said. "Is anyone with her?"

"I think Sean is taking her back to the house. She's not wanting to go, but there isn't much she can do here."

Jennie nodded. "Are you going too?"

Shelagh nodded. "You can come with us."

"No. I'll stay until they find Gram." Jennie watched intently as they sifted through the rubble. Gram could be under all of it. "I'll walk you to the car," she said to Shelagh. As they approached the Keegans' car, William drove up.

"I heard the explosion," he said. "Is everyone all right?"

"Me da's been hurt," Shelagh told him. "And Helen is nowhere to be found."

Panic lit his eyes. "Helen is . . . missing?"

"I don't know," Jennie answered. "She might still be in there. Maybe you can check. They might talk to you."

William nodded and hurried over to an officer.

Jennie turned back to the Keegans. Sean was sitting behind the wheel, Catherine in the passenger seat.

"Did I hear you say Helen is missing?" Catherine rasped.

"We'll find her," Jennie said with more assurance than she felt. She leaned in through the open window to grasp Catherine's hand.

"Where are Thomas and Bridget?"

"On their way to the hospital. Thomas was hurt. . . . Not badly."

"Take us to the hospital, Sean. I'll not be going home just yet."

"But, Grandie—"

"No arguments."

"Da won't be happy about this."

"You let me worry about your father. Just do as I say."

Sean shrugged. "What about you two?"

Jennie shook her head. "They still haven't found Gram. I'll stay with William."

"I'm coming." Shelagh opened the car door. "I want to be with Da."

When they drove off, Jennie started back to where William was still talking with the police. She'd taken only a couple of steps when he came back to her. He seemed relieved.

"They don't believe she's in the building. That's all they can tell me."

Jennie frowned. "Then she must have gone after the guy who left the bomb. Maybe she thought she could catch him."

"How long has she been gone?"

Jennie glanced at her watch and was surprised at the time. "Forty-five minutes." She didn't want to think about what so much time passing could mean. If Gram had tracked down the guy who planted the bomb, she could be in more danger than if she'd been inside.

William must have been thinking the same thing, because he looked as though someone had hit him. "I'm going to have a look around, then." He started to get into his car but then paused and glanced at Jennie over the roof. "Would you like to come?"

Jennie nodded, glad he'd asked. It saved her having to insist. She dove into the car before he could change his mind.

They drove up one street and down the other and into the alleys but saw no sign of Gram. Jennie felt sick. They went back to Mulhaney's Pub, or what was left of it, to talk to the police again. They still insisted Gram had not been inside the building when the bomb went off. No one had seen her come out, and neither Thomas nor Mr. Mulhaney could remember seeing her inside the building before the bomb went off. Jennie's stomach had gone beyond feeling sick. It was hard as stone. She felt numb, as though everything happening around her was happening to someone else.

William told the officer who had questioned Jennie about Gram's history as a police officer. "She may well have gone after the culprit."

"We'll have a look around, then." The officer placed a hand on William's shoulder. "You'd best be going on home. We can handle it from here."

William agreed. "He's right, Jennie. There isn't much more we can do here."

Jennie didn't want to go and suggested they stop at the hospital to see Thomas. "Maybe Gram's been taken there as well."

The medical center was small but efficient. On the off chance that Gram had been injured and brought in amidst the confusion, Jennie and William checked with the receptionist. No one else had been brought in. They found Bridget in the waiting room. She wrapped her arms around each of them, Jennie first, then William.

"How's Thomas?" Jennie asked.

"He's fine. The doctor said for once we can be happy he has such a hard head." Bridget gave Jennie a wistful smile. "He'll be going home soon."

"Will you need a lift, then?" William asked.

"Thank you, no. Catherine and the children are here. Sean will take us home."

"Do you think we could talk to Thomas?" Jennie wrapped her arms around herself. "We still don't know what happened to Gram."

Bridget bit her lower lip. "The nurse said she'd be bringing him out soon."

She'd gotten the last of her statement out when a nurse wheeled Thomas out to where they all stood. "Here you are, Mrs. Keegan."

The nurse nodded and said good-bye, teasing Thomas about being a terrible patient. As soon as the nurse left, Jennie asked him about Gram.

"She was helping us get people out." He wagged his head back and forth. "I lost track of her. Wish I could help."

"Might she have gone back to the castle?" Bridget asked.

"Not without me," Jennie insisted.

"She might have if she thought you'd be there."

"She has a point, Jennie," William said. "It's the one place we haven't looked."

———

No one else was about when William and Jennie entered the castle. Jennie had seen several lights on but didn't know which rooms they were in or who belonged to them. Once inside, they hurried upstairs to Gram's room.

"Gram isn't here."

William placed an arm around Jennie's shoulders. "We'll find her, Jennie. I'm sure of it. I'll see to it myself if I have to. You should try to get some sleep."

When William left, Jennie sank onto Gram's bed. "Where are you, Gram?" Lying back, she closed her eyes. "God, please let her be okay. Please." She fell asleep like that, praying and imagining Gram being there with her.

It was still dark when she awoke to a pounding noise. Jennie shot off the bed and flung open the door.

16

Out in the dimly lit hallway, Jennie stood, listening again. Nothing. Had she only imagined the noise? She rubbed her eyes and peered at her watch. Only two in the morning—which meant she'd been asleep for little more than an hour.

Jennie went back inside. Since she was still dressed, she toyed with the idea of walking into town to check with the police. But they'd probably be gone by now. And going out alone at night wouldn't have been the smartest move she'd ever made. Instead, she went into the bathroom, washed her face, and went into her room for a nightgown.

Her senses sharpened. Something wasn't right. Someone had been in her room.

Probably Megan or a maid, straightening up. Jennie opened the drawers and made a quick check. Nothing was missing that she could tell. A faint scent of perfume wafted from the drawer. Strange. Why would anyone go through her things?

Jeremy hadn't gone to the pub. Maybe he had taken the opportunity to snoop around. But why would he do that?

Could someone have been looking for something? As far as Jennie knew, she had nothing at all worth taking. Had they gone through Gram's room as well? She'd have to ask Gram to check.

But what would she and Gram have that someone

would be after? Could it have something to do with their investigation into Liam's death? Had Gram uncovered something incriminating? Maybe the killer thought so. Jennie shook her head. The idea seemed farfetched in light of the people they'd interviewed. She couldn't imagine any of them as a killer. Still, hadn't it been an older person who'd planted the bomb? True, it could have been a younger person impersonating a doddering old man. Had someone found something in Jennie's or Gram's room and planted the bomb to kill them both? Jennie frowned. The bomb had been planted shortly after William left. Could he have done it?

"That makes no sense at all," Jennie muttered. "He's the one who wanted Gram to investigate his father's death."

What about Declan? Maybe. He could have called his father to get him out of the pub and make certain he was safe, then pretended to be an old man setting down what anyone watching would presume to be a liquor bottle. But why?

Jennie shook her head again. She hated the way her mind worked sometimes—plugging everyone into the suspect role. But she needed to rule people out. Declan was a nice guy, but he'd been at the graveyard when she'd been locked in the old tomb. He hadn't come to the party, but then, neither had Jeremy or the duchess. William had supposedly been called away. Declan hadn't even been born when his grandfather died, so he couldn't have killed him. Neither Declan nor Maude wanted William and Gram to investigate Liam's death.

Maude had been a young mother with a three-year-old child. Somehow Jennie couldn't see the petite woman hefting a grown man and tossing him over the wall. Could she have pushed him? Jennie made a mental note to go up to the walkway and see for herself where he had died. "But not tonight," she said aloud. *In the morning*, she promised herself.

She drew in a deep breath. Maybe Gram would be back by then.

Jennie pulled on her nightgown and slipped between the cool sheets. Leaving the lamp beside the bed on, she wrote her suspicions in her journal until the book and pen fell and the door of her mind closed.

Jennie awoke around six the next morning to the sound of water running and Gram singing another Irish song.

Gram is here? Had last night been a bad dream? Had yesterday even happened? Or was Jennie dreaming now? She eased out of bed and crept to the bathroom. She eased open the door. "Gram?"

The singing stopped.

"Is that you?"

The shower curtain moved and Gram stuck her shampooed head out. "You were expecting Frank Sinatra? I know my voice is low, but—"

"Last night . . . the bomb. You weren't there."

"Let me finish up here, darling, and I'll tell you the whole story."

Several minutes later, Gram came into Jennie's room. Jennie flung her arms around her grandmother. "You don't know how glad I am to see you."

"I'm sorry you were so frightened. William told me how you'd looked everywhere for me."

"Where were you?" Jennie still couldn't believe Gram was actually there.

"Buried in the basement. I was going through the rooms making sure everyone was out. I'd gone into the storage cellar when the bomb went off. Part of the floor and the stairs collapsed, and I was trapped and cut off from the main part of the building. It sealed me in for a good long while. I finally managed to dig my way through enough of the rubble to be heard."

"You should have come in to wake me up when you got here," Jennie scolded.

"I only just arrived. William came to pick me up at the hospital."

"You called him?"

"Didn't have to. He came back to help after he dropped you off. He helped rescue me."

"I was afraid you'd gone after the bomber."

"It was more important to get everyone out of the building."

"I know." Jennie hugged Gram again. "Do you think the bombing has anything to do with your investigating Liam's death?"

"Oh, Jennie. I very much doubt it. The authorities told me there have been several random bombings recently outside of Northern Ireland. Apparently this is similar in that the suspect was wearing a brown overcoat and left the bomb in a paper bag."

"Hmm. It just seems like more than a coincidence to me. I mean, look at all the things that have happened. The note, you almost being run down, the farmhouse being torched, and now the bombing. It has to have something to do with your investigation. What else could it be?"

"Ordinarily I'd say you were right, but you have to remember that our suspect list is confined to people who were old enough and strong enough and who had motive, means, and opportunity. From what we've learned so far, I'm leaning toward the suicide theory."

"Doesn't there have to be motive there too?"

"True. We know Liam had his share of unhappiness, but it wasn't like him to shirk his responsibilities. William refuses to believe he'd leave his wife and son."

Gram pulled Jennie into another hug. "But let's not worry about that right now. I want to celebrate being alive. First, though, I'd better get some sleep. Then I'd like to take a drive. We'll see if Catherine wants to come along.

Think you can find something to do for the next few hours?"

"I'll manage."

They both ended up taking a nap. Jennie could finally relax, knowing Gram was safe in the next room. The maid woke them around ten as they'd asked, and after a quick brunch, Jennie and Gram set off in William's Roadster. He'd gone to the horse races with a friend and didn't need it. Catherine had gone into Callaway with Bridget to do some shopping. She'd left a note to that effect on the kitchen table, asking Jennie and Helen to join them.

Gram considered it but decided to stick with their original plan to do some sight-seeing.

Jennie didn't care where they went. She just felt relieved to be leaving the area. When they reached the outskirts of town, Gram headed south along the coast.

"Gram, did you notice anything out of place in your room when you came in?"

"I noticed someone had been lying on my bed."

"That was me."

"I suspected as much." Gram winked at her.

"No, I mean like someone had gone through your stuff."

Gram leaned over to squeeze her hand. "I didn't see that anything was missing. To be honest, I was too tired to notice anything. Why?"

"I think someone searched our rooms—well, mine, anyway. Maybe it was just a maid straightening up, but . . ."

"That makes sense."

"I think someone was snooping around, maybe trying to find something."

"I don't have anything of interest. Do you?"

"No. Just the genealogy stuff I printed out at the monastery. I know someone had gone through my drawers."

"Well, perhaps we have a nosy maid. I'll speak to William about it."

Jennie didn't want anyone getting into trouble, especially if that person was Megan. "No, don't. I might just be imagining it. I was worried about you."

"Yes, but you have a good eye and good intuition."

"Nothing was taken that I could tell."

"What do you say we not talk about any of that now and just enjoy the day together," Gram suggested.

"Okay, but I have one more question."

"What's that?"

"When I was up in the attic the other day looking at your mother's stuff . . ."

Gram gave Jennie an I'd-rather-not-talk-about-it look. "I'm glad you're finding it interesting."

"I know you're not ready to deal with that yet, but I wanted to tell you what I found."

"Which is?"

"Some linens and two diaries."

Gram adjusted the sun visor. "I had no idea she kept one. I don't remember her ever writing in a journal or keeping a diary."

"Maybe she didn't when she was older, but she did when she was young. I haven't had a chance to read it yet. I thought we could maybe read it together."

"That would be nice—maybe in a few days." Gram's tone didn't match her smile.

"You don't sound very enthusiastic. Didn't you like your mother?"

"I loved her." Gram gave Jennie an odd look. "I don't think she loved me. Oh, she did all the motherly things, I suppose, but her heart wasn't in it. I imagine it had something to do with Dad's dying so young. She never remarried and had to be terribly lonely. As I look back on it now, I wonder if she may have been suffering from depression."

"Can I ask you one more question?"

"Depends on what it is."

"The genealogy report I got at the monastery."

"Sure."

"I think there's a mistake on it. Did you know you were born only six months after your parents got married?"

"What?"

"I checked the dates on the genealogies for both Mary and Hugh. They both have your birth date as six months after their wedding."

Gram rubbed her forehead. "There has to be a mistake somewhere. The dates on my parents' wedding certificate and my birth certificate clearly show I was born ten months after their wedding."

Gram hesitated and then added, "I'm certain that's correct. For one thing, my mother was never promiscuous. She felt very strongly about remaining a virgin until you were married. At least, that's the lesson she drummed into my head. My father was an honorable man as well." She gave Jennie a wan smile. "Sounds like I'm over-defending them, doesn't it."

Jennie shrugged. "Happens all the time these days."

"It happened then too, but I doubt that would have been the case with my mother. Having a baby out of wedlock was shameful back then. If she had gotten pregnant, you can bet the marriage would have taken place the moment she found out. Her father would have seen to that."

Jennie found the discussion uncomfortable. Somehow thinking of her own great-grandmother having sex at all, let alone before marriage, seemed totally out of line.

"Ah, Jennie." Gram hauled in a deep breath of fresh air. "Isn't Ireland grand? I know we have a lot to discuss, but the day is too lovely to waste on the past."

Jennie settled back and let the wind toss her hair around. She let the wind take her concerns and questions as well and sweep them across the hills.

An hour into their drive, they stopped in a small town to fill up with gas. While they waited for the petrol, Gram and Jennie went into a store to get drinks. Gram got some coffee and Jennie a lemonade.

From there they drove up a narrow, winding road to the top of a hill overlooking the ocean. Some of the cliffs rose hundreds of feet above the water. At several points they got out to take pictures and marvel at the rugged landscape. The road itself gave them some frightening moments as it hugged the hills on one side and the sheer drop-offs on the other. Gram kept her speed down on the curves, but even so, Jennie had moments of near panic as she imagined William's bright yellow car soaring off the edge.

Gram seemed to understand Jennie's fears. They weren't groundless, after all. Both she and Gram had been in near-fatal accidents where their cars had careened off the road. Once in Florida a truck had come up on them from behind, forcing them off a bridge and into the water. Another time Jennie had been bumped from behind while on a road in the coastal mountains.

Gram reached over to pat Jennie's leg and reassure her that the roads were perfectly safe. There was no truck following them and no reason to be afraid. Then, on a downhill run, Gram speeded up, and the wheels squealed as they took a sharp corner.

"You took that curve kind of fast, didn't you?" Jennie wasn't normally into telling others how to drive, especially adults. But then, Gram usually drove well.

"Hold on, Jennie! The brakes are out."

17

Gram maneuvered another curve, then another. She jammed the car into low gear to slow it down, and it did for a few seconds. The road twisted and turned, with deep ravines on one side and thick trees on the other. Gram pumped the brake, but her efforts did nothing.

"Hang on." Gram gritted her teeth and narrowly missed a guardrail, sending gravel spewing out behind the wheels. Thankfully, after several more turns, the road evened out and took an uphill turn. Jennie blew out the breath she'd been holding and released her white-knuckle hold as the car slowed and came to a stop. Gram turned the car sideways in the road and put it in park. One finger at a time, she released the steering wheel and then leaned her head against it.

"That was fun." Gram waited until her breathing slowed to a normal rhythm and then leaned over to take Jennie's hand. "You okay?"

"Yeah. Pretty scary. Not as bad as the other times, though."

Gram shook her head and inched the car off the road. After getting out, she popped the hood.

Jennie climbed out and came around to where Gram stood.

"I don't believe it." Gram pointed to a gash on one side of the brake line. "Someone has deliberately sabotaged us."

"We could have been killed."

"I think that's exactly what someone wanted. What I can't understand is when it was done. The car was fine when we left the castle. At least, I assume it was." Gram frowned and examined the line again. "The brake line has been cut but not severed, which would cause the brake fluid to leak out slowly. Whoever did it wanted us to be well away from town when it happened."

"Do you think they meant for the brake fluid to drain out while we were up on the cliffs?"

"It would be impossible to pinpoint exactly when we would run out completely. And on a car this old, there are no gauges to let us know."

"We only stopped once. Could someone have tampered with it then?"

"I suppose it's possible." Gram closed the hood on the car and straightened, her gaze scanning the countryside. "Looks like we have two choices. We can walk to that farmhouse we passed and call for help, or we can wait for someone to come along. Unfortunately, this isn't a very busy road, but I imagine someone will come by eventually."

They started walking, and a few minutes later a farmer in a pickup truck slowed, drove by, stopped, and backed up. Gram told him what had happened, and he offered them a lift to his farm, just a few miles away. Since there was room for only one in the cab, Gram insisted on riding in the back with Jennie. At the farmhouse, the man's wife offered them coffee and dessert while they waited for a tow truck.

They got back to the castle around four that afternoon. William came outside to meet them. Glancing from Gram to the truck, he asked, "What happened?"

"Brakes went out." Gram opened the tow truck door and slid to the ground.

William gasped. "You've got to be joking. Mac serviced the car just before you took it out."

Jennie jumped to the ground. "We were up near the cliffs when it happened."

"Fortunately," Gram added, "we were able to slow down on an uphill grade." Gram handed the tow truck operator some money after he detached the car from the tow bar.

"Thanks. Appreciate the help."

"Glad to be of service, miss. Sorry for your troubles." He tipped his hat, got into the truck, and rumbled away.

William ran a hand through his hair. "I can't believe this. I'll have a word with Mac. There's no excuse for not checking the brake fluid. I'll pay for the tow, of course."

"It wasn't an accident, William." Gram slipped an arm through his as they headed toward the front door.

"What on earth are you saying?"

"Someone deliberately cut the brake line. I'm not certain when—perhaps here, or perhaps while we were stopped to fill up with gas."

"Mother and Declan were right. I shouldn't have asked for your help in finding my father's murderer. I should have left sleeping dogs lie."

"You couldn't have known. I must admit, I'm surprised myself. Makes me wonder if you may be right after all and that someone did kill Liam. I was leaning against it. But with the attempt on our lives last night at the pub and today, I'm not sure what to think. Of course, one incident may have nothing to do with the other. And there's a very good chance nothing that's happened has anything to do with our investigation into Liam's death. After all, I did get the threat while I was still in the States. I may have an unseen enemy. One thing for certain, I have to send Jennie home."

"I'm not going," Jennie mumbled under her breath.

"I'm puzzled, though," William went on. "If by chance there is a link between the investigation and these events, who could be responsible?"

"Perhaps we should do some serious thinking about

the suspects. It would have to be someone who knew Jennie and I were going on an outing this afternoon."

"I'm afraid that leaves Jeremy, my mother, and me, the staff, of course, and the Keegans. I certainly didn't do it. And the others would have no reason."

"I'm sure no one here tampered with the brake line," Gram reassured him.

"Maybe someone saw us leave town and followed us," Jennie suggested.

Gram turned around and waited for Jennie to come inside. Putting an arm around her, she said, "You're most likely right, darling. I'm furious about this. It's one thing to want to kill me, but to endanger my grandchild . . . William, we must find out who did this. I'd like to talk with the authorities. I'm going to report this incident. I'd also like to know if the police have any leads on the bombing last night, as well as the hit-and-run."

William shook his head. "I can't imagine anyone resorting to such evil tactics. And if they were only after you and Jennie, why would they endanger the lives of so many people?"

Helen sighed. "I wish I knew."

"I'll put in a call to the inspector. We'll have a talk with him this evening. Perhaps he can come here."

A few minutes later, William hung up the phone. "That's strange. The inspector is already on his way. Declan just rang him up." William paused to sit down, a stunned look on his face. "Seems my son has found a body in the carriage house."

18

The brake lines and bombing all but forgotten, Jennie followed Gram and William to the carriage house. Hoping she wouldn't be ordered to her room until all the excitement had passed, Jennie stayed a safe enough distance behind. Gram wouldn't want her to see a dead body. Jennie didn't want to see it either, but she did want to know what was going on.

Distant sirens split the air. "What happened?" William demanded as they stepped inside.

Declan's face was pasty white. He was sitting in the driver's seat of his car with the door open. He groaned. "What are you doing out here?"

"I just talked to the police and was told you'd discovered a body."

Declan shook his head. "They told me to stay away from the crime scene—I think that goes for you as well."

"Where is the body?" Gram asked. "Do you know who it is?"

"Inside." Declan pointed to the closed garage door. "It's Mac."

"No!" William leaned against the car. "How did it happen?"

"I have no idea. I just got home, and when I opened the garage door, he was lying in there on the floor in a puddle of blood. I thought he'd been hurt. I got out to see if I could help, but . . . he's dead."

Jennie shuddered at the thought. Poor Declan. "And poor Megan."

"Jennie." Gram didn't look happy to see her there.

Jennie thought for sure Gram would send her back to the castle. Instead, Gram came over and wrapped her arms around Jennie. "This is no place for you. I—" She stopped.

Jennie made the same connection Gram must have. Mac had worked on William's car. He had access to it. Had he cut the brake line?

"It's not possible." William seemed to understand where their thoughts had gone as well. "Mac wouldn't have sabotaged the car. He's been with us for thirty years."

"What are you talking about?" Declan got out of the car and closed the door. Before they could answer, an officer drove up, and behind him came a medical response vehicle.

"Ah, Mrs. Bradley. We meet again." The inspector pushed his glasses back against his nose as he extended his hand to Gram. "So nice to see you again. I must say, when we met last night I had no idea what a celebrity you were. I'd be pleased to have your input on this investigation." His smile faded as he turned his attention to Declan. "You have found a body?"

Declan nodded. "In there. I opened the garage and there he was. I checked him—thought at first he'd been injured, but he's dead. He's been shot."

The inspector nodded. "My crime lab people should be here momentarily. In the meantime I'd like to have a look"—he nodded at the door—"if you would be so kind."

Declan pushed the button on his garage door opener.

Jennie closed her eyes as the door opened. She still half expected Gram to make her go back to the castle, but she didn't. Gram seemed focused only on the body and looking for evidence. Though she'd been retired from the police department for several years, she hadn't lost her investigative skills or her propensity for getting involved.

"Maybe you'd better go back to the castle." It was William, not Gram, who spoke.

Gram turned back to Jennie at the suggestion. "William's right, Jennie. You'll have nightmares for weeks."

"Please, no." Jennie bit her lip. "I won't get in the way. And I won't look at him."

Gram sighed. "All right, then, but stay well back."

Jennie stepped back several feet, blocking her view of the body entirely. William took one look at the corpse and came back to where she stood, ashen faced, like he might be sick at any moment. Jennie's stomach felt queasy too.

"Nasty business, this," he murmured. "What do you make of it?"

"I don't know. Maybe it has something to do with the brake line being cut. He might have found out who did it and they shot him."

"Mmm." William's gaze moved back to the garage but darted away again. "Frighteningly close to home, isn't it? We rarely have trouble of any sort here, you know.

"I shouldn't have asked Helen to look into my father's death," William went on. "Obviously we've stirred things up. I daresay no one we've spoken to could have been responsible for it. Perhaps the stories are true and it was a ghost."

"A ghost didn't kill Mac, Willie," Gram had come back to them while he was ruminating. "He was shot in the chest at close range. I think it may have been someone he knew. There were no signs of a struggle. Shot sometime around noon—not long after we left, Jennie. There's a bloody shoe print next to the body, but I suspect it's Declan's."

Two medics brought out a stretcher with Mac's covered body on it and placed it in the rear of the ambulance.

"We should have more details once the autopsy is done."

The inspector, who'd been studying the garage floor, straightened and walked toward them. "Do you have any idea who might have killed him?"

"None," William answered. "He was well liked in town. Never a bit of trouble for us. Always did his job." He shrugged. "I don't know what to make of it."

"He was here when we left," Gram said. "He'd been working on the Bentley. Didn't seem bothered by anything. He waved us off and told us to have a good time. Said we might need gas since he hadn't had time yet to take it into town to fill it."

"Nothing amiss, then."

"Nothing at that point. But two hours later, our brakes went out." Gram rubbed the back of her neck. "No brake fluid, and the line had been cut."

"Your brakes?" The inspector raised a dark, shaggy eyebrow.

"On William's car. The leak was slow, but enough to assure we'd run out in the midst of our trip."

"Are you suggesting he may have cut the line?"

"Mac wouldn't have done that," William put in.

"Jennie suggested he may have discovered who did and was killed to silence him."

The inspector gave Jennie a cursory glance. "Indeed. It's as good a premise as any, I'd say. Mrs. Bradley, do you know of anyone who'd want you and your granddaughter dead?"

"No. Unless it's somehow connected to a fifty-six-year-old murder." Gram and William briefly filled the inspector in on the investigation they'd been conducting. "It makes little sense, though. William told me he hadn't spoken to anyone about asking me, yet I received a threat before leaving the States. There must be something else."

"Hmm. It appears you've opened Pandora's box." The inspector sighed. "William, I'd like to speak with your other employees. Perhaps you could make a list for me." He hesitated, then added, "While you're at it, write down the names of anyone who knew of this investigation of yours. And for now, at least, let me handle that as well. In the meantime, I suggest you watch your step."

"We have a security system in the castle," Declan offered. "Perhaps I should hire a body guard until you discover who's responsible."

"Good idea. I know a couple of men who could use the extra money."

To Jennie's surprise, Gram didn't argue and seemed relieved to have the inspector taking over. Jennie fully expected Gram to refuse a body guard. Gram was well versed in karate and could handle herself in just about any situation. Jennie had seen her in action more than once. She suspected Gram was taking precautions for her. Gram looked worried when she turned to Jennie and said, "That goes for you too, darling. No probing or questions."

"But . . ." Jennie didn't see why she couldn't talk to people about it. She'd helped police track down killers before. *And almost gotten yourself killed*, she reminded herself.

"Mac has been murdered," Gram insisted. "I know how hard it is to stay out of it, but we must. We don't know but what Mac's death and the near misses we've had aren't connected. I don't want you doing any investigating." She looked directly into Jennie's eyes. "Do you understand?"

Jennie nodded.

William cleared his throat. "Inspector, if there's nothing else, I'll go inside. We'll need to tell Mac's family. And I'll make up that list for you."

The inspector nodded. "I'll know where to find you if I have any more questions."

William turned to his son, who was leaning against his car, face in his hands. "Declan, are you coming?"

He shook his head. "The inspector asked me to stick around."

Jennie wanted to stay and watch the crime scene investigators go over the scene, but Gram's steady pressure on her elbow propelled her forward. She thought about asking to stay with Declan but decided to go along peacefully. It wouldn't do any good at this point to argue. She had to admit that she was well out of her league in trying to solve a murder. There were just too many unknowns. Still, she couldn't help wondering if Mac's death was somehow connected with Liam's even though it was fifty some years ago.

Megan greeted them as they came in. "Mr. Kavanagh, the duchess wants you to come up immediately. She's very upset, wanting to know why the police and ambulance are here. Mum and I would like to know as well."

"Yes. I'll need to talk with your mother." William settled a hand on her shoulder.

"Is it Mac, then? He's been hurt?"

"I'm afraid it's more serious than that."

Megan went to get Beatrice from the kitchen. When they returned, William told her that her husband had been shot and killed.

Beatrice wailed, and Megan pulled her into an embrace. After a few moments Beatrice looked up at them. "Whyever would anyone want to shoot Mac? And wasn't himself the kindest man we've ever known?"

"He was," William agreed.

"And wouldn't he do anything for anybody?"

"Aye. That he would."

A bell rang.

"That'll be the duchess." Megan glanced at her mother and then said to William, "She'll be wanting to talk with you. I'll stay with me mum if it's all right."

William nodded. "The inspector is here. He'll be coming in to ask questions." He heaved a deep sigh. Turning to Jennie and Gram, he said, "I'd appreciate your coming up with me to tell her. Mother's always had a soft spot in her heart for Mac."

William started up the stairs, and Gram and Jennie followed. Remembering how the duchess had watched them when they'd first arrived at the castle, Jennie wondered if the duchess had seen anything that might help solve the murder.

"It's about time you came. I asked Megan to bring you around twenty minutes ago." The duchess was lying on a Victorian chaise lounge, her legs covered with a knit throw. "What's happened? I saw the police and ambulance from my room. I hate growing old. Would have come to see for myself, but my arthritis is giving me fits today."

"Bad news, I'm afraid." William went to her and, taking hold of her hands, said, "Mac's been shot."

With a sharp intake of breath, she pulled her hands away and drew them to her chest. Bringing a lace-trimmed handkerchief out of its hiding place in her sleeve, the duchess touched it to her eyes. After a moment she seemed to compose herself. "That poor man. Is he going to be all right?"

"I'm sorry to say he didn't make it," William said sadly.

"How could anyone have done such a thing?"

"That's what the police are trying to find out," Gram said.

William then told her all they knew of the murder.

"Oh, William." The duchess lifted a shaky hand to her chest, the jeweled rings catching the window's light. "However shall we manage without him? Does Beatrice know?"

"Yes. I spoke with her before coming upstairs."

"How is she?"

"She'll manage. Megan is with her."

"Such a frightful thing. And here in our very own home. Do you suppose the killer is still about?"

"I don't know. I imagine the inspector will have his people search the grounds."

"Of course."

Jennie scanned the large sitting room. There were three large windows, and the chaise sat in front of the center one. While William comforted his mother, Jennie went to the window to the right. From it she could see the town and the woods, as well as the road coming into the estate and the carriage house and stables.

When no one asked the question Jennie had on her mind, she decided to ask it herself. "Did you see anything? Maybe someone coming into the place or leaving?"

The duchess looked blank for a moment.

"Jennie." Gram gave her a stern frown. "This isn't the time."

"It's all right, dear. I imagine the inspector will want to know." Maude wagged her head back and forth. "I've seen no one on the grounds since earlier today when you two left. I've been dozing off and on all day. The pain pills make me sleepy, you know." She frowned, touching her hanky delicately to her nose. "Oh, I did see Thomas earlier, not long before you left. He was talking to Mac. You don't suppose . . ." She shook her head. "Gracious. What am I saying? He and Mac were dear friends. Thomas often comes over to help with the cars. They were working on William's strange little sports car earlier."

"That was before we left?" Gram asked.

"Yes. About thirty minutes, actually. I remember because I had that long before my next dose."

"Gram, you don't think Thomas cut the brake line, do you?" Jennie folded her arms and turned away from the window.

"Of course not. What reason could he possibly have to want us dead?"

"Brake line? What on earth are you talking about?" The duchess clutched at her chest, looking as if she might be about to have a heart attack. Jennie wished she hadn't said anything.

Gram explained, saying the brake fluid had run out. "We had a few scary moments, but nothing to concern yourself about. As you can see, we're fine."

The duchess drew in a wheezy breath. "How horrid. How absolutely horrid." Looking up at William, she said,

"I was afraid something like this might happen, what with your obsession over your father's death. The ghosts are angry again."

"Mother, the ghosts have nothing to do with this. Mac was shot point-blank with a real gun and real bullets. Now, you mustn't upset yourself with all of this ghost nonsense."

"You're right. It . . . it's just hard not to wonder about them. You've narrowly escaped being killed two times in a row."

"Me? It was Helen and Jennie who have been in danger."

"Are you certain? They may not have been the intended victims. It was only by God's grace that you weren't in that pub last night and driving the car today."

God's grace? Jennie turned back to the window. The duchess had a point. William could have been the intended victim, or he could have been the instigator. Could William have planted the bomb and sabotaged his own car, knowing Jennie and Gram would be taking it into the hills? Could Mac have found out or even been in on it? Jennie hated to think of William as a suspect. He certainly hadn't killed his father, but he had opportunity to plant the bomb and cut the brake line. Jennie pinched her lips together. Why? He had no motive that she could see. And he seemed to love Gram. He wouldn't have sent a note telling her to stay away. Would he?

Love could do strange things to people. Make them crazy. Could he have been holding a grudge all these years? Jennie had recently seen a movie where this guy fell in love with a woman, and when she went to break it off, he killed her. If she didn't want to be with him, he wouldn't let her be with anyone.

Jennie sighed. *You're letting your imagination run away with you.* William would have gotten over Gram years ago—enough to marry someone else and have a son. Besides, Jennie couldn't see him as a killer. He was just too kind.

Declan had apparently finished talking to the inspector and was on his way inside. Jennie's imagination stirred up visions of him planting the bomb, cutting the brake line, and killing Mac, but again she couldn't see a motive.

The duchess leaned back on her chaise again as William said, "This has been a traumatic two days. I want you to rest now before dinner. I'll have Megan bring your tray up."

"Yes, thank you. I don't think I can manage the stairs."

"Do you need anything else?" William asked.

The duchess closed her eyes. "Would you close the blinds and pull the drapes, please?"

"I'll get them," Jennie offered. She moved slowly from one to another, watching the inspector talk to two other men in an official vehicle that had just driven up.

"William?" The duchess sounded weak and tired. "You'll talk to the inspector for me, won't you? I don't see how I could possibly speak with him today."

"I'll take care of it."

Reluctantly, Jennie closed the last of the draperies. *End of Act Two.* She hesitated for a moment before walking out of the darkened room with the others.

19

Back downstairs, Declan seemed to look through Jennie and Gram. "I'm so sorry this had to happen. If you'd like to go somewhere else, I'll be glad to pay for your accommodations."

"You'll do no such thing," Gram said but then hesitated. "Unless you want us to leave . . ."

"No. Not at all. It's just . . . this isn't much of a vacation for you."

Gram placed a hand on his arm. "You needn't worry about us, Declan. We'll be fine."

Declan nodded, a faraway look in his eyes. "Has anyone seen Jeremy?"

No one had.

"Hmm. He wasn't in his room. Perhaps he's gone to visit the Keegans. Well, if you do see him before I do, tell him I need to talk to him. I'll be up in the library."

While Gram went to help William make a list of people to talk to, Jennie went to her room, where she picked up her latest novel and began reading. But reading was hard to do when thoughts of the dead man, the fire, the bombing, and their near-death experience with the brakes kept popping into her head. Not to mention the note and the incident with the white van. Jennie had to stop thinking about it. Gram had made it clear that she was to stay out of the investigation completely. Jennie had promised she wouldn't get involved—and she wouldn't—but somehow she was having trouble convincing her brain of that.

Jennie thought briefly about working on her genealogy report but didn't feel like getting up.

After only a few minutes, Gram knocked on her door. "Shelagh's here. She'd like to see you." Jennie set the book aside and went to the door.

"Hello, Jennie," Shelagh said shyly. "I wondered if you'd like to spend the night with me." She hesitated. "Da's had a talk with Sean, and he's promised not to pull any shenanigans. We could go up in the attic and look in Mary's trunk if you'd like."

The last part of the invitation enticed Jennie. Well, not just that. The castle had lost its appeal, and Jennie wasn't looking forward to spending another spooky night there. She could sleep with Gram, of course, but after all, she was nearly seventeen years old.

Jennie glanced up at Gram. "Is that okay?"

"Yes. I've spoken to Bridget on the phone. They'd be pleased to have you."

"I'll go then. Are you sure you don't mind our looking through your mother's things without you?"

"Not at all. You're doing me a favor, actually. William and I have talked, and we'll be looking through some papers Liam left behind. Might give us a clue as to what happened to him."

"I thought you were going to stop investigating his death."

Gram shrugged. "It's more for Willie's sake, really. He's terribly upset about the whole thing. Thinks maybe we'll find something among his father's papers that will shed some light on all of it."

Jennie nodded. "I hope so. Gram, is there any chance that William could have . . . you know. . . ?"

"Willie?" Gram chortled. "You can't be serious."

"He had opportunity. The only thing I can't find is motive."

"I'll save you the trouble of looking for one. Willie wouldn't hurt anyone."

"I hope you're right. But be careful, okay?"

Gram pulled Jennie into a hug. "I'll be fine. We have a guard coming this evening. Besides, we don't know for certain that we were the intended victims. As Maude said, whoever cut the brake line on William's car may not have known we were taking it out. And if William hadn't been called home the night of the party, he'd have been there with us."

"I suppose you're right."

"We'll be safe enough as long as we stay close to home." Gram's assurance didn't quite ring true. "Have a good time, you two." Gram gave Shelagh a hug and Jennie another for good measure and then left the two girls alone.

Jennie packed a change of clothes in her small bag and retrieved her toothbrush and other essentials from the bathroom.

"Did you have a chance to read Mary's diaries?" Shelagh asked.

"No. With all that's happened today, I completely forgot." Going to the nightstand, Jennie took out the diaries and stuck them in her backpack. "I'll bring them. Maybe we can read them together tonight."

Shelagh beamed. "I'd like that. Just think, Jennie. We'll be reading the very words Mary wrote when she was a young girl. I love to read about the history of Ireland. And Mary lived that history."

Jennie brightened as well. It would be fun to read about Mary's life.

"Did you walk over?" Jennie asked as they went outside.

"Yes. I hope you don't mind. I can carry your bag."

"It's not heavy." Jennie put both arms through her backpack and settled the strap of her overnight bag onto her shoulders.

They walked along the road through the estate, as it

was the quickest way back to the house. As they walked, Jennie told Shelagh about the adventure with William's car and about Mac's death.

"Da told us about Mac. Very hard for him. Mac was a good friend. We all liked him. Da did a lot of work for him—especially these last few years."

"Why's that?"

"Mac had rheumatism. Sometimes his back hurt so bad he could hardly stand up. Poor man. Sad to see him all bent-over like that."

Jennie had seen Mac only once, and he was bent—over a car. She'd thought him to be in his seventies, but it was hard to tell. She hadn't seen him walk, though. Or had she? The man who'd left the bomb in front of the pub had been bent-over as well.

"How old was Mac?"

"I couldn't tell you for sure. Da would know."

Old enough to have killed Liam? But then, who killed Mac? Jennie thought it best not to share her musings with Shelagh.

"How's Jeremy's ankle coming along, then?" Shelagh asked. "I was hoping to see him when I came to get you, but he didn't seem to be anywhere about."

"I don't know. Haven't seen him since just before we left for the pub last night." Jennie remembered Declan's question about whether anyone had seen him. "Declan thought he might have gone to your house."

"He didn't. Do you suppose he's all right?"

"I wouldn't worry." Then Jennie added, "The castle's a big place. He could be anywhere."

"Hmm. Must be fun living in a house so big that no one would even know if you were there."

"You could hide out all day and not have to do chores. But then, Jeremy probably doesn't have any chores." Jennie didn't express the rest of her thoughts—that Jeremy could have had something to do with the brakes, the bomb, and the shooting. *But why? He doesn't have a motive either, does he?* She couldn't think of one, but he might have seen something. Jennie made a mental note to talk with him about it.

Shelagh opened the door for Jennie when they reached the house. Jennie stepped inside and felt immediately at home. Unlike the castle, it felt warm and cozy. The table had been set, and Bridget had a smudge of flour on her chin.

"Welcome, Jennie. We're happy you could come."

"That we are," Catherine said. She stood at the stove, stirring a steaming pot of something. "Our meals are not so grand as at the castle, but they're warm and filling."

Jennie drew in a deep breath, savoring the aroma of some sort of meat and fresh-baked bread. "Smells wonderful."

"Aye, it does." Bridget closed the oven door and gave Jennie a hug.

It was something her mother would do, and Jennie felt an unexpected wave of homesickness—which was silly, since she'd been gone less than a week. She blinked back tears.

"There now, are ye crying? Did we do something wrong?" Bridget cradled Jennie's face in her hands.

"No," Jennie sniffed. "It's just . . . you reminded me of my mom, and . . ."

"Ah." Catherine stopped stirring the soup and put the lid on it. "Sure and aren't you a wee bit homesick. You miss them. Of course you do. Your mum must be missing you as well. She called not more than ten minutes ago. I told her you'd call her back as soon as you arrived."

"She called? Here? Is everything all right? Are they still coming?"

Bridget laughed. "Everything is fine." Turning back to the stove, she said, "Shelagh, be a darling girl now and tell your da and brother to come in for supper."

"Do I have time to call home?" Jennie asked.

"We'll wait to eat until you are finished. The phone is in the sitting room."

Jennie punched in the numbers for an overseas call. It would be midmorning back home in Portland.

"Jennie!" The voice belonged to her cousin Lisa.

"Hey! What are you doing there? Did you forget I was gone?" Jennie teased.

"Nope. I'm baby-sitting Nick while our parents go out to brunch and a matinee."

"What are they seeing?"

"Not sure. Our fathers are complaining because it's a chick flick."

Jennie laughed. She missed them all more than she'd thought possible. Even though she sometimes complained about taking care of Nick, she almost wished she were there to do it.

"Are you coming to Ireland with my folks and Nick?" Jennie asked.

"Maybe. So how is it there?"

"You wouldn't believe me if I told you."

"Wait. Let me guess. You and Gram have gotten yourself involved in another mystery."

Jennie groaned.

"I'm right, aren't I?"

"Um . . . yes. But don't tell Mom and Dad, okay? I don't want them to worry or change their minds about coming."

"Why would they do that?"

"Well, there's been some trouble." Jennie decided not to go into the details. "We're fine. In fact, we've been staying in a castle. You'd love it."

"A castle? How did you manage that?"

"This old friend of Gram's offered. Though tonight I'm staying with the Keegans."

"Sounds fun. What are they like—Shelagh and Sean, I mean."

"Nice . . . Well, they have their moments. You'll see

what I mean when you get here."

"Who said I was coming?"

"Come on, Lisa. You can't fool me."

Lisa sighed. "So much for the surprise. You're no fun at all. How did you know?"

Jennie laughed. "You are just too obvious. Acting like you didn't care if you came or not. I know you, Lisa Calhoun. If you couldn't come, you would be really upset."

"Hang on." A moment later Lisa was back. "Gotta go. Your mom wants to talk to you."

"Hi, honey. We sure miss you around here." Mom's voice almost made Jennie cry again.

"I miss you too."

"How's everything?"

"Good. Ireland is so beautiful. We're right on the Atlantic coast. Some parts look like Oregon."

"We'll have to make this quick. Just wanted to let you know I love you and miss you. Oh, and we'll have a surprise when we come."

"You mean Lisa?"

"She told you?"

"I guessed."

"Well, all is not lost. We have another surprise as well."

"What?"

Mom chuckled. "You'll have to wait until we get there."

Jennie sighed. "Mom, how could you do that to me?"

"We know how much you like mysteries." Mom laughed again, and there were some voices in the background. "That was Dad, Kate, and Kevin saying to tell you hi. Dad says to stay out of trouble."

Jennie hesitated a little too long.

"Jennie? Is there a problem?"

"Mom, you worry too much. Gram and I are fine." Jennie thought it best not to relate their adventures to this point. No sense in getting her all upset. "There's so much to tell you."

"I'm anxious to hear all about it. Love you. Talk to you soon."

"Bye, Mom. Tell everyone I love them." Jennie hung up the phone and went back to the kitchen just as Shelagh came in with Sean and Thomas.

Bridget brought a steaming kettle to the table.

Dinner was as delicious as it smelled. Gram and Jennie's own mother had often made Irish stew. Jennie had even made a version herself, but none of their efforts matched Bridget's. Jennie told her so. "Thanks for inviting me."

"You're always welcome here, Jennie." Catherine leaned over to pat her arm.

Thomas offered a prayer, thanking God for their good fortune in still having their home and for bringing everyone out of the explosion alive.

They fell into a comfortable silence then, each intent on eating. Sean hadn't said a word to Jennie. She wondered if he'd gotten in trouble for the stunt they'd pulled on her in the graveyard. *Serves him right*. Still, she hoped he wasn't mad at her. Thomas seemed sullen too, and Jennie imagined he was grieving for his friend Mac. She wanted to talk about the murder, ask questions, but decided it wasn't the best topic for a dinner conversation.

Catherine broke the silence by asking, "How is your family, Jennie?"

"Good." Jennie broke a piece of warm corn bread and drizzled honey over it.

"They're still coming, then?"

"Yes, and they're bringing Lisa."

Shelagh cheered. "Wasn't I hoping they would do just that? Mum says I look like Lisa. Do you think so?"

Jennie nodded. "You're both very pretty. I have a picture in my backpack. I'll show it to you later."

Someone knocked. Sean and Thomas both stood.

"I'll get it." Thomas set his napkin on the table. Adjusting his suspenders, he opened the door. "Inspector, come in." Thomas moved aside to admit him.

Removing his hat, the inspector stepped in and nodded to everyone at the table. "Sorry to bother you during your meal."

"No trouble at all," Thomas assured. "What can we do for you?"

"As you know, we're investigating Joseph McIntyre's death."

"Aye. 'Tis a terrible thing. Mac was a good friend."

"It appears that a gun is missing from William's collection."

"William's gun? You'll not be thinking William killed Mac?"

"He's not a suspect. At the time of Mac's death he was at a racetrack in County Cork. We're trying to locate Jeremy. The boy appears to have run off."

20

Shelagh gasped. Sean gave her a look that could stop a buffalo. Their reaction sent Jennie's stomach to the floor.

"You're thinking the boy shot Mac?" Thomas ran a hand through his hair.

"Too soon for that. We're just wanting to question him. Have you seen him, then?"

Thomas shook his head and turned toward the table, his gaze moving from his own children to Jennie. "Any of you seen Jeremy?"

"Not for a while," Sean answered, his face turning red as his freckles.

Shelagh's eyes widened as the inspector waited for a response from her. "I've not seen him since yesterday."

They weren't lying, Jennie decided. But they weren't telling the entire truth either. What were they up to? She felt certain they knew more than they were telling, but neither Thomas nor the inspector seemed to notice.

"How about you, Jennie? Have you seen him?" Jennie had been so intent on Sean and Shelagh, Thomas's question hit her like a smack alongside the head.

"Not since last night," Jennie said. "He'd hurt his ankle and didn't want to go to the party at the pub."

"All right, then." The inspector backed out. "I'll let you get back to your supper. Sorry to bother you."

"No trouble at all."

Thomas came back to the table, and Jennie felt certain

163

he would light into his kids for lying. Sean and Shelagh were staring at their stew again. Thomas dipped a big piece of bread into his bowl, sweeping up the remains.

Jennie's appetite had withered away to nothing, but she finished her stew anyway. Her cousins were hiding something, and Jennie had a hunch that something was Jeremy. She could hardly wait to get them alone.

After dinner Sean went back outside with his father to finish up the chores while Jennie and Shelagh helped Bridget and Catherine with the kitchen.

As they worked, Jennie wondered about the connection between the missing gun and Jeremy. She hated to think he could have been involved, yet it certainly was a possibility. He was unhappy. His parents had divorced, leaving him torn in half. He was living with his father yet wanting to be with his mother. Kids involved in shootings had become all too common in the U.S. Jennie shuddered at the thought. Could Jeremy have taken the gun? If so, was Mac the only victim? Would there be others? Had Jeremy gone on a shooting spree?

"Would you like to see Molly's babes?" Shelagh's question yanked Jennie's mind away from her macabre thoughts.

"What?"

"Molly's babes. Da says I get to name them and raise them. They'll be milkers like their mum. You can help me pick out names."

Fifteen minutes later, Shelagh pulled Jennie outside and handed her a pair of black boots. "You can use Mum's Wellies. You won't want to go into the barn without them."

Jennie glanced around, making sure they were alone. "You know where Jeremy is, don't you?"

Shelagh jumped. Pressing her lips together, she pulled on her boots. Casting furtive looks around, she let out her breath in a whoosh. "How did you know?" she whispered.

"I'm good at reading people." Jennie stood, forcing her foot deeper into the boot. "You and Sean weren't that hard to read. In fact, I'm surprised the inspector didn't catch on. Where is Jeremy?"

"If I tell you, promise you won't say anything to *any-one*?" Shelagh stressed the last word.

"I can't make a promise like that. What if he has the gun? What if he's killing people?"

Shelagh shushed Jennie and took another look around. "Jeremy wouldn't shoot anyone. How can you say that?"

Jennie lowered her voice. "He may have killed a man, and if he has a gun . . . Shelagh, he could be dangerous."

"Jeremy? Dangerous? Don't be silly. He doesn't have a gun. And even if he did, he wouldn't use it on anybody."

"How can you be so sure?"

"Haven't I known him for years? And isn't he my neighbor and a dear friend, now?" Shelagh pulled at Jennie's arm as they neared the barn. "Don't say anything to Da, please."

"I want to see Jeremy—talk to him."

"All right. But later, after Mum and Da have gone to bed. Just promise you won't tell."

Jennie nodded. "For now. Is he in the barn?"

Shelagh shook her head.

Jennie frowned. "But earlier you asked me about him. . . . I don't understand."

"I only just found out. Sean told me before dinner." Shelagh led Jennie to the back of the barn and into a stable in the far corner. "Aren't they the loveliest little things?"

Jennie pushed her concerns about Jeremy to the back of her mind, her face splitting into a grin as she looked into the stall. "Mollie's a goat?"

"Of course." Shelagh giggled. "What did you think she was?"

"I don't know. A cow, I guess." Jennie leaned over to pet the goat's silky black head and run her hand down her shaggy coat. "Your dad said her milk made good cheese."

"Aye. Goat cheese. We've several like her. She's the best breeder."

Molly bleated when Shelagh picked up one of her babies—a smaller version of Molly, with a whiter coat.

"They're so cute."

"You can hold one if you like. Molly won't mind too much."

Jennie picked up the remaining kid and brought it to her chest, letting it nuzzle her neck. "What are you going to name them?"

"I don't know." Shelagh pulled an apple from her pocket and held it out for Molly to nibble.

"How about Sweet and Sugar?"

Shelagh giggled. "Sure and they're grand names, Jennie. How did you come to that?"

"Their coats remind me of spun sugar, and they are sweet."

"Sweet and Sugar it is, then."

When they got back to the house, Shelagh and Jennie took candles up to the attic and began looking through photo albums and a box of loose photos that had belonged to Mary. They set the albums aside to take downstairs and began sorting the pictures in the box, separating out the professional portraits. The girls made a game out of matching baby pictures to their grown counterparts. One of the photos was of a strikingly handsome young man whom neither of them recognized.

"Are you sure he's not related?" Jennie asked.

Shelagh shrugged. "I don't remember seeing him in any of our albums."

"He must be a relative." Jennie traced a finger over his dark hair and eyes. "He looks like my dad."

"We'll have to ask Aunt Catherine. She'll know." Jennie nodded and placed the photo of the mystery man in the growing stack of pictures Jennie planned to take downstairs. Most were of Gram growing up.

After nearly two hours of sitting cross-legged on the attic floor, Jennie stood and stretched. She rubbed her sore shoulders and yawned. Looking at her watch she asked,

"What time do your parents go to bed?"

"Around ten."

"We still have almost an hour."

"Let's go downstairs and have a snack. There should be some tarts left. We can have them with cream."

Sean was in the kitchen devouring one of the tarts when Shelagh and Jennie came downstairs.

Bridget smiled at them. "I was just about to call you. Ye'll both want one, won't you?" Without waiting for an answer, she scooped up some whipped cream and placed a large dollop on each of the tarts.

"Looks good." Jennie pulled out a chair and slid into it. Her mouth watering, she picked up a spoon and broke into the flaky crust.

"Are Da and Catherine not having some?"

"Already have. Da's gone to bed. Poor man, with Mac dying and all . . . Makes for a hard enough day. Grandie's gone to bed as well."

"Grandie bakes the best desserts." Shelagh dug into her tart. "Fairly melts in your mouth."

"Catherine made this?" Jennie asked.

"She did." Bridget sipped at her tea. "I don't know what I'm going to do with that woman. I keep telling her to rest, and what does she do? Same as she's always done. You'd think a broken leg would slow her down."

"Well, it has some, Mum. She's only started baking again since Helen and Jennie arrived."

Sean picked up his plate and took it to the sink. Giving Bridget a peck on the cheek, he said, "Night, Mum."

"Off to bed so early?" She ruffled his hair.

"I have some math problems to work out."

"I'll see you in the morning, then."

"How about you, Shelagh? Are you needing to get ready for school next week?"

"I've already done my homework."

"There's a good girl." Bridget placed her own tart on

the table and sat across from the girls. "Did you find anything interesting upstairs?"

"We had a good time going through the pictures." Shelagh paused to slip a piece of tart and cream into her mouth. "Mmm. Is it not the best you've ever tasted, Jennie?"

"It is."

"Show Mum the picture of the man who looks like your da, Jennie. Maybe she can tell us who he is."

Jennie had set the photos on the floor near the landing. She went to retrieve the photo and handed it to Bridget.

"Hmm. He does look familiar. I can't place him, though. You'll want to ask Grandie or your grandmother in the morning."

They talked with Bridget for several more minutes before she announced that she, too, was going to bed.

She'd been gone for only a few minutes when Sean snuck down the stairs.

He didn't look happy to see them. "Thought you'd gone to bed too."

"I told Jennie we'd take her to see Jeremy."

"You told her?" He scowled as he opened the refrigerator and took out some meat.

"And didn't she guess, Sean Keegan. You told her yourself with that guilty look on your face. But you needn't worry. She's promised not to tell."

Jennie started to correct Shelagh but decided against it. If Sean suspected she might go to the authorities with what she knew, he'd never agree to take her.

Sean eyed Jennie warily. He didn't trust her. And Jennie didn't blame him.

"All right, then," Sean said finally. "Help me fix his dinner."

A few minutes later they were walking through the field carrying flashlights, which they hadn't turned on. The moon provided enough light in the open pasture.

"Where is he?" Jennie asked.

"Cemetery." Shelagh hurried to catch up.

Jennie stopped short. "I am not going into that place again. You must think I'm pretty stupid if you think I'm falling for your tricks again."

"We're not playing a joke on you. Jeremy is hiding in the gardener's shed." Shelagh turned to her brother. " 'Tis true, is it not, Sean? Jennie's afraid we're out to trick her."

"He's there, all right. You think I'd be bringing this food if he wasn't?"

"See."

Jennie almost laughed. "Oh well, if Sean says so, then it must be true."

"Are you two coming or not?" Sean turned around and continued walking backward.

"Coming." Shelagh hooked an arm around Jennie's and tugged her forward.

Jennie relented.

When they reached the cemetery, they stayed low and walked alongside the fence until they reached a place where some of the ancient rocks had crumbled away. Sean snapped his flashlight on, and Jennie followed the two of them, determined not to let her cousins out of her sight. At least with them in front, she wouldn't have to worry about their pulling some kind of prank again.

They wove their way through the headstones toward the old tomb in which Jennie had been locked. She shuddered at the memory. "Why would he hide here? I thought you were afraid of the monster."

"There's no monster," Sean admitted. "We just told you that to scare you."

"Gee, thanks. So you did lock me in?"

"No, but I know who did. The gardener. I talked to him this morning. He felt bad—didn't know anyone was in there."

"How could he not have known? I yelled loud enough to wake the dead." Jennie still wasn't convinced.

"Wouldn't have been able to hear you," Sean said. "He's deaf."

Jennie frowned. "I don't get it. Does he know Jeremy's here?" She couldn't imagine an adult going along with Jeremy's staying there.

"He's gone to Galway." Sean shrugged. "His mother took ill. With him gone, this seemed the perfect place."

"Oh yeah." Jennie wondered what her cousins and Jeremy had for brains.

Sean knocked lightly. The door opened, and a hand shot out, pulling Sean in.

"It's about time you got here," Jeremy growled. "I'm starving."

"Sorry. Couldn't get away any sooner."

When Jeremy saw the girls, he sank to the floor. "What did you do, bring the whole town?"

"Of course not." Shelagh sounded hurt. "Jennie's staying overnight, and—"

"It's not their fault." Jennie hunkered down beside Jeremy. "The inspector came by the Keegans' place at supper. He was looking for you. I noticed Sean's and Shelagh's reaction. I don't think anyone else did."

Jeremy tore into the sandwich. "So they're looking for me. I'm surprised they even noticed I was gone."

"That's not fair. Your father asked about you this afternoon." Jennie paused and then added, "One of William's guns is missing."

"And they think I took it? Figures."

Jennie looked up at Sean. "Does he know about Mac?"

"I haven't had a chance to tell him."

Jeremy swallowed, his gaze shifting from one to another. "What?"

"Mac's dead. He was shot—possibly with the missing gun."

Jeremy groaned. "They think I did it?"

"They want to question you." Jennie stood and folded her arms.

"I didn't shoot him—or anyone. I liked Mac."

"When did you last see him?"

Jeremy shrugged and took another bite of sandwich. "Yesterday, I guess."

Friday, Jennie thought. *The day before the brakes were cut.* "When did you leave?"

"This morning," Jeremy answered. "What's with all the questions? You're worse than my father."

"I'm sorry. I'm just trying to figure out what happened. You picked a lousy time to run away."

"I'm not running away. I'm leaving Ireland for good. Tomorrow morning I'll hitchhike into Shannon and fly home."

"Oh, that's brilliant." Jennie paced back and forth in front of him. "The police are looking for you, Jeremy. The airport is the first place they'll look."

"Jennie's right." Shelagh dropped to her knees. "Wouldn't it be for the best if you talked with the police?"

"Who asked you?" Jeremy growled.

Shelagh jerked back as though she'd been hit. "All right, then. Get yourself arrested. See if I care. Come on, Jennie. Let's go home."

Jennie hesitated at the door. "Running away isn't the answer, Jeremy. It never is."

"You don't have a father like mine."

"Sure and don't you have a very nice father, Jeremy Kavanagh." Shelagh glowered at him. "He's a kind man with a heavy load. Da says he admires the man, having to raise a boy on his own."

"Your father loves you. Anyone can see that." Jennie sighed. "Don't do this, Jeremy. It will break his heart."

"A lot you know."

Jennie swallowed hard. He had her there. She really didn't know much about their relationship. She'd been basing her comments on her own parents. "Come on, Shelagh, let's go." When they got to the fence, she stopped. "Should we wait for Sean?"

"He'll be a while, I'm sure. Poor Jeremy."

"You like him a lot, don't you?"

Shelagh didn't answer right away. "I do."

"Does he know that? Maybe if he did, he wouldn't be so eager to leave Ireland."

"I doubt it would matter. He's of a mind to leave, and there'll be no stopping him." Shelagh stared at the ground, and when she looked up, there were tears in her eyes. "Besides, it does no good to think about being his girlfriend. My parents would never allow such a thing."

"Because you're Catholic and he's Protestant?"

Shelagh nodded.

"What made him decide to leave now?" Jennie asked. "Did something happen?"

"Had a big blowout with his da. Jeremy has been wanting to go to the U.S. for a long while. And hasn't his mum been making promises?"

"Declan isn't mean to him or anything, is he?"

"You mean does he beat on him?" Shelagh shook her head. "Not at all. He's not stern enough, me da says. Jeremy's spoiled."

"No kidding."

"Oh, Jennie, sure and aren't we in for it now. The lights are on at the house."

"Looks like the police are back." Jennie eyed the flashing lights.

"What do you suppose that's all about?"

"Maybe they discovered we were gone. Maybe they read your faces like I did and suspect you can lead them to Jeremy."

"Aye, but wouldn't they have followed us to the cemetery, then? You don't suppose something's happened to Grandie?"

They broke into a run.

It wasn't Catherine. The police car was pulling out

when they got there. Bridget sat at the table in her bathrobe, crying.

"Mum." Shelagh rushed to her side. "What's wrong?"

Bridget shifted her teary gaze from one to the other. "They've arrested your father. They think he killed Mac."

21

"It can't be true." Shelagh sent Jennie a desperate look. "Da wouldn't kill anyone. What will we do?"

Jennie didn't know what to say. It didn't seem likely that the police would take Thomas in without just cause. The duchess had told them that Thomas was working on the car with Mac. Could the two of them have been collaborating? Had Mac and Thomas both cut the brake line?

Jennie was jumping to conclusions. There was nothing to connect the tampered brake line, or any of the other things that had happened, to Mac's murder. For all she knew, they could all be unrelated incidents. Jennie knew Thomas hadn't planted the bomb or set the fire. Mac could have. But why? Thomas had been as shocked by the bombing as anyone. *Still, they arrested him.* Jennie frowned. *They wouldn't do that unless they had a reason.*

"Did they find the missing gun?" Jennie asked.

"I don't know," Bridget sobbed.

Shelagh stood behind her mother, hands on her shoulders. Panic replaced the shock in her eyes. "What will we do, Jennie?"

Jennie took a deep breath. "Make tea." She needed thinking time. She needed sleep. And most of all, she needed to talk to Gram. Jennie put some water on to boil. Did Gram know about Thomas's arrest? Had something happened at the castle? Had the police uncovered some new evidence leading them to Thomas?

Jennie wished now she hadn't left the castle. *If you hadn't*, she reminded herself, *you wouldn't know about Jeremy*. Thinking about Jeremy took her in a whole other direction.

Jennie knew her grandmother would be focusing on the most serious problem, which for the moment would be Jeremy. They'd be searching for him. Looking at Shelagh, Jennie said, "We have to tell Declan about Jeremy."

"Jennie, you promised."

Bridget sniffed. "What are you talking about? You know where Jeremy is?"

"It isn't fair. Gram and Declan and William—and who knows all—will be frantic." Jennie glanced at her watch. It was almost midnight.

"What's going on?" Sean came in with Jeremy trailing behind.

He'd come back on his own. Jennie almost hugged him, and Shelagh certainly looked as if she wanted to.

The story of Thomas's arrest tumbled out again. Sean tore outside, determined to go straight to the authorities and demand answers. "He's done nothing wrong."

Jeremy stayed in the kitchen. "I'm sorry, Mrs. Keegan."

"Where have you been?" Bridget demanded. "The police were looking for you as well. I don't understand what's happening here. It's like the devil has loosed his most frightening demons on us." Making the sign of the cross, she murmured, "Lord have mercy."

The teapot whistled. Jennie poured hot water over tea bags in a large pot and set it on the table to steep while she took several cups from the cupboard.

"Thank you, Jennie." Bridget wrapped her hands around the cup. "Perhaps this will clear our heads and put things into perspective."

Drinking the warm tea seemed to calm everyone, including Sean, who'd stormed around the yard for several minutes before coming back inside. Jennie assured them that if Thomas was innocent—and they all believed he was—he'd be home by morning.

"I don't know. Seems more serious than that. It's the middle of the night." Worry etched Sean's face with lines that made him look much older than sixteen. "Why couldn't they have waited until morning?"

"Because a man's been murdered." Jennie set her tea on the table. "There's been a bombing. Someone seems determined to kill Gram and me."

Sean tipped his head down, looking intently into his tea as though he might find answers there.

"I'll call Gram. She'll find out exactly what's going on." Jennie's gaze drifted to Jeremy. "You've decided to go back to the castle?"

He nodded. "Sean and I talked after you left. It was pretty stupid of me to leave. I didn't take the gun, and I sure don't need that hanging over my head. Dad's not such a bad sort. He just doesn't understand." He took a sip of tea. "That's not quite true. I left because I was mad. My mother sent a letter saying I wouldn't be able to come live with them after all. It would be best if I stayed with my father. I thought maybe if I went there and talked to her in person, she'd change her mind."

"I'm sorry." Jennie couldn't imagine how it must have felt to have his mother reject him again. Just hearing the words and the tone of his voice twisted Jennie's stomach into a double knot.

"I acted like a jerk. Got mad at Dad instead of her. I thought he'd put her up to it. I decided to go to the U.S. and see for myself. Dad tried to smooth it over. Told me she loved me in her own way. Maybe she does." Jeremy glanced at Jennie. "Something you and Shelagh said back there got me to thinking. Sean helped me sort it out. It's better to stay in a place where you're loved and wanted than to try to force yourself on someone who doesn't care. I've been a real jerk lately. I'm sorry."

"Does that mean you'll be staying here in Ireland,

then? Permanently?" Shelagh offered a hopeful smile. Her admiration for him was obvious.

He sighed. "I'll be staying if Dad will still have me. He's probably ready to ship me back to the States."

"Oh, I doubt that, Jeremy." Bridget ran a thumb up and down her cup. "Declan is a good man. He does his best to provide a good home for you. He'll do right by you for sure."

"Yeah, well, there's still the deal with the missing gun and Mac's death."

"We need to get you back to the castle right away." Jennie pushed her chair back. "I doubt your dad or William or Gram will be asleep, with you gone. We can give them some peace of mind and find out what's going on with the investigation at the same time. Knowing my grandmother, she's way ahead of the inspector."

"Don't go, Jennie," Shelagh pleaded. "You were going to stay here."

"If I stayed, we'd be going to bed now anyway. I'll stay another night when things get settled."

"Jennie's right, luv." Bridget placed a hand on Shelagh's arm. "Better that she and Jeremy go back to the castle. Sean, be a dear boy and give them a lift."

———

Jeremy's homecoming turned into a celebration. Declan and William took turns hugging him—after they'd scolded him properly for running off they way he had. Even the duchess came downstairs to welcome him. Jeremy apologized for giving them so much grief. They didn't even demand an explanation, nor did they ask him about the missing gun.

Jennie, unable to contain herself any longer, had to find out. "The sheriff came by during dinner looking for Jeremy and said that one of William's guns was missing. He thought maybe Jeremy had taken it."

William seemed surprised by her statement.

"I didn't take it," Jeremy assured them. "I didn't kill Mac."

"We know you didn't." Declan settled an arm across his shoulders. "You complicated matters by leaving when you did. But we never once connected you with the gun or Mac's death."

"They found the gun in a duffel bag in a trash bin behind the stable," Gram offered.

"Did you know they've arrested Thomas?"

"Yes, the inspector said he intended to. Apparently Thomas's prints were on William's car. And the duffel bag belongs to him. His prints are all over that too."

"They found his prints on the gun?"

"No. That had been wiped clean."

"That makes a lot of sense," Jennie quipped. "Wiping a gun clean and then stuffing it into a bag with your prints all over it."

Gram smiled. "My thoughts exactly. William and I will talk to the inspector again in the morning."

They all headed off for bed. Jennie was far too tired to think about castle ghosts, death threats, or even murder. Her only thought before she drifted off was that she and Shelagh had never gotten a chance to read Mary's diaries.

———

The next morning the sun shone bright with promise. Gram came in at ten and announced that they'd be going to church.

"I thought you were going to talk to the inspector about Thomas."

"We've already done that. They're not convinced." Gram sighed. "They seem certain they have their man. They're thinking Thomas was working with Mac—or had hired him to kill me."

"Why?"

"Well, the theory is that Thomas was afraid I'd come back to claim the farm."

Jennie didn't tell her that she'd come up with that idea earlier herself. "But I looked at Thomas's handwriting when we first came. It didn't match."

Gram raised her eyebrows. "The inspector told us this morning that they'd determined who sent the note and who'd tried to run me down."

Jennie frowned. "Mac?"

Gram nodded. "They make a pretty good case, but I simply can't believe Thomas had a hand in any of it."

Jennie wasn't sure what to think. She went to church with Gram in Declan's car and was surprised and pleased when Gram drove on into Callaway to go shopping after the service. By late afternoon, when nothing bad had happened, Jennie wondered if the authorities might be right. They drove back, stopping at the farm to see how the family was holding up.

Jennie felt terrible for her cousins, but there was nothing she or Gram could do except pray.

They left around six, and after an elegant dinner at the castle, William talked Gram into going for a walk. Jennie just went upstairs and got ready for bed. Were they finally safe? Had Mac and Thomas been working together? In a way, Jennie wanted to believe it, yet she couldn't. Something just didn't feel right.

Jennie doused the light and, after peering out her window for several minutes, crawled into bed. This would be the first night since their arrival that she'd be in bed before midnight.

———

The next morning, everyone except the duchess, whose arthritis was giving her fits again, had arrived for breakfast early. Jennie came in as they were finishing their meal.

"Are you sure you want to go to school today, Jeremy?" Declan set down his empty coffee cup. "What say we both play hooky and go riding." He glanced around the table.

"All four of us." Declan's mood was understandably good, with Jeremy's coming home, but his cheerfulness seemed foreign in light of the events of the past few days. Still, Jennie thought a horse ride sounded wonderful.

William grunted. "Have you forgotten, Declan, that we have a murder on our hands? Not to mention a neighbor falsely accused."

"It's okay, Dad," Jeremy said. "I really should go to school. We can ride when I get home."

That surprised Jennie.

Declan nodded, disappointment in his eyes. "I suppose it's for the best. I'm a bit behind. But I want to let you know, Jeremy, that you come first. Family comes first. I've forgotten that lately, and I'm sorry for it."

Jeremy rose and settled a hand on his dad's shoulder. "I know. Hey, Jennie, do you want to ride this afternoon? I'll talk to Sean and Shelagh on the way to school. Okay if they come too, Dad?"

"Absolutely."

"Sounds good to me." Jennie waved Jeremy off and went to the buffet to pick over what was left of breakfast: scrambled eggs, Canadian bacon, orange juice. She put a slice of bread into the toaster and, while she waited for it to pop up, set her plate on the table.

Gram set her napkin aside and turned to William. "If you're ready, I suppose we should go into town and see if we can spring Thomas." Turning to Jennie, she said, "Would you like to come?"

Jennie shook her head. "I've had enough excitement for a while. Think I'll stay here and read. Maybe explore a little. Do you mind if I hang out in the library?"

"Not at all," Declan and William said together. "You've the run of the castle. Just let the duchess know you'll be wandering about so she doesn't think we have an intruder."

Jennie grinned. "I'll do that. Thanks."

"If we get back early enough and don't have any complications, maybe I'll join you." Gram pushed her chair in. "I love exploring."

"And I'll take you on a tour," William added. "Something we should have done when you first arrived. Not that we've had time."

"I'll leave you, then." Declan drained his orange juice and wiped his mouth on the white cloth napkin. "I should be home around three."

A few minutes later, Jennie sat in the dining room alone. She'd finished her first helping of eggs and bacon and went to the buffet for a second. She liked the silence—the aloneness—but at the same time felt uneasy. She passed off the feeling as being skittish. And no wonder. *A man has been killed. The murderer could still be in the castle.*

22

Probably not. Jennie figured the killer would want to be as far away as possible—unless he hadn't finished the job. Jennie closed her mind to that possibility. She wasn't really alone in the castle anyway. The duchess was upstairs. And Jennie could hear Beatrice and Megan working in the kitchen. Megan came in to gather the dishes the others had left.

"Hi." Jennie grinned at her, relieved and glad for the company.

"Oh, Jennie. Hello. I didn't realize you were still here. Please don't let me rush you." Megan took an armload of dishes and headed for the door.

"No problem. I'm almost done."

"Are you sure you don't mind my cleaning up around you?"

"Not at all. In fact, I'll help you." Jennie took the last bite of bacon and began stacking plates.

"You'll do nothing of the sort. You're a guest. The Kavanaghs wouldn't like it."

Jennie laughed at the protocol. "None of them are here except the duchess, and she's upstairs."

"All right, then. I suppose it would be okay. Mum and I would be happy for the help. Especially today. She should be resting, you know, with Da gone. But no, she's insisting she'll be better off working."

"What about you?"

"Oh, I'm agreeing with her, you know. I'm younger, and he wasn't me real father."

"I didn't know. Are your parents divorced?"

"Me own da died of cancer when I was a mere child of twelve."

"Did he work here too?"

"Oh no. We lived in Ennis. He was a construction worker. Died of asbestos in the lungs. When he died we lost everything. William, kind heart that he has, gave us jobs here in the castle."

"And your mother met Mac."

"Aye. The rest is history. Now she's lost Mac. 'Tis going to be terrible hard on her."

"Megan, did Mac have any enemies?" Jennie wasn't sure why she'd asked. Habit, she guessed. Or maybe she just wanted to find a way to prove Thomas was innocent.

"Oh, I suspect everyone has a few. I knew of none. He was always kind to Mum and me." Tears shone in her eyes.

Jennie apologized for asking and finished clearing the table and buffet. When she offered to help with the dishes, Beatrice made it clear that Jennie was a guest and that she didn't allow guests in the kitchen.

Jennie gave up and went to her room. After brushing her teeth, she felt at odds. Should she read or explore? *Read*, she decided. And what better time did she have to take a look at Mary's diaries? She took out the books and unfolded the linen. Opening one, she began to read:

June 1, 1942. Summer has come. Mother's flowers are sure to be in bloom. Would that I could be there to see them. It's more than happy I should be on this summer day. For the first time I feel the tiny life stirring inside me.

That tiny life was Gram. Jennie thought it strange to be reading the thoughts of a woman who would soon be giving birth to a woman who was now a grandmother.

How I love this babe and even more its father. Would

that I could tell him. But I dare not. For ours is a love that can never be. Instead of happiness, I feel nothing but fear and shame. What will happen to us, little one? I can't go home. They would never understand. My babe will be born without a father.

Jennie lowered the book and stared at the window opposite the bed. *So it's true. Gram was conceived before Mary married Hugh O'Donnell. Was Hugh the father? Or was there someone else?*

Jennie read again. Mary talked about staying at a boardinghouse in Galway and working there to earn her keep, and how she longed to see her parents but didn't dare go home. People wouldn't understand. A month later she'd met an old friend and distant cousin, Hugh O'Donnell, who'd come into Galway on business. He was kind and seemed to take a liking to the quiet, sullen woman Mary had become. He made her smile again. He found excuses to come into town, and after a few weeks passed he asked her to marry him. Mary struggled. Should she tell him the truth and risk losing him? Or should she come clean and tell him about the babe? Mary decided that if she and Hugh were to have a life together, it had to be built on honesty. One evening while they were walking around the park, she confessed that she was carrying another man's child. She refused to tell him who the father was.

For a moment she was afraid he would walk away, but after a moment's silence, he turned her toward him and kissed her. *"The past doesn't concern me,"* he'd said. *"Only the present and the future."* He declared his love for her, and in a few days they married. They came back to Callaway and moved into the house where Gram was born a few months later.

Jennie had tears in her eyes when she set the book down again. What a beautiful love story. But Mary still hadn't mentioned who Gram's real father was or how she'd come to be pregnant. Jennie supposed she should leave it be. Mary didn't seem obliged to mention the man, not even in her diary. She didn't think it mattered, but it did—to Jennie, at least. If Hugh O'Donnell wasn't her great-grandfather, who was?

Jennie went into the bathroom to get a tissue and blow her nose. Though she hoped to learn more, she was tired of sitting and needed some exercise. An hour had passed since breakfast. She went to the window, wondering if Gram and William had come back. Jennie saw no sign of William's car but peeked into Gram's room just in case they'd come in without her seeing them.

Feeling at odds again and restless, Jennie made her way downstairs. The only voices she heard were coming from the kitchen, so Jennie headed there. Beatrice and Megan assured Jennie that William and Gram hadn't yet arrived, but that they had tea ready for them.

"We'll be taking tea up to the duchess, Jennie," Megan said. "I'm sure and she'd be pleased if you would join her."

The tea tray with its scones and clotted cream and jam made Jennie's mouth water. "If you're sure it would be okay with her."

"Oh yes. The duchess loves her company."

"Would you like me to take it up?"

Megan waved her hand. "You'll do no such thing."

"Well, at least let me open the doors."

The duchess welcomed Jennie like a seldom seen old friend.

When she'd settled the tray on a table, Megan left.

"I'm so glad you've decided to join me, Jennie. I get lonesome sitting up here in my ivory tower." She laughed. "But then, when you get to be my age, people come to see you more out of duty than out of true friendship. Not that I'm complaining. Duty is better than nothing."

Jennie wasn't sure what to say but needn't have worried. The duchess went on without hesitation.

"Tell me, Jennie, who coerced you into having tea with me this morning?"

Jennie grinned, deciding to be honest. "Not duty. Actually, the scones looked good. And I was taking a break."

The duchess laughed again. "Then scones you shall have, my dear. Would you do me the honor of pouring? My hands are too shaky these days. I have Parkinson's, you know. Not severe, my doctor says. I can still hold a cup of tea."

Jennie poured them each a cup and set a scone on both plates. "I can't believe I'm hungry. I ate a huge breakfast."

"You're an active child."

"I haven't been very active this morning. I've been in my room reading."

"Ah. I used to love to read when I was your age. Did you know that a lot of famous writers hail from Ireland?"

"I know of a couple. William Butler Yeats and George Bernard Shaw."

"Ah yes. Yeats. Do you know his work?"

"We read some of his stuff for school."

The duchess went on to list several others: Jonathan Swift, Oliver Goldsmith, Sean O'Casey, and James Joyce.

"Who were you reading, dear?"

"No one famous. My great-grandmother Mary."

"Mary O'Donnell?" The cup and saucer clattered as the duchess set down the cup. "You see, there it is again. The tremors come at the oddest times."

Jennie reached for a napkin to sop up the tiny spill.

The duchess reached for her scone. "I didn't know Mary was a writer."

"It's a diary, actually. I found them in the Keegans' attic." Jennie started to tell the duchess about Hugh not being Gram's father but decided not to. Gram didn't even know that herself. "She wrote about marrying Hugh and having Gram. It's a romantic story."

"It must feel odd to read another woman's diary. Especially from so long ago. I kept a diary once—filled it with my deepest, darkest secrets. When I got married, I burned it."

"Why?"

"So my children and grandchildren wouldn't read it. Some thoughts are meant to be private."

Jennie frowned. "You don't think I should read Mary's diaries?"

"Them? You have more than one?" The duchess picked up her cup and saucer again.

"I've found two so far."

"And have you read them both?"

"No. I've almost finished one of them. I think I've read them out of order, because the one I'm reading didn't start until she met Hugh."

"Ah. Has your grandmother seen them?"

"Not yet."

"Did you know that Hugh worked here for some time? Does she mention us at all?"

"Only once, where she talks about moving back to Callaway and Hugh working for the Kavanaghs."

"Hmm." The duchess gazed out the window. Turning back to Jennie, she leaned back against the cushions of her chaise. "And what else have you discovered in the attic? I hope you don't mind my asking, but I used to love poking through the attic when I was a young girl. It's such a personal way to discover family history, don't you think?"

Jennie smiled and nodded. "It is interesting. We— Shelagh and I—found an old trunk that had a sticker from Paris on it. We thought maybe Hugh and Mary had gone there for their honeymoon." Jennie brightened, realizing that the duchess might know. "Do you know?"

"Oh my. It was such a long time ago. But yes, it seems to me Hugh did take some time off." She smiled. "That must be it."

Jennie took a sip of tea. "I found some linens. Gram said Mary made a lot of them herself."

"What a lovely keepsake." The duchess closed her

eyes, and for a moment Jennie thought she'd fallen asleep. "You're lucky to have them. The fire could have destroyed the entire house—including Mary's treasures."

"I hadn't thought of that." Jennie set her cup down. "You don't suppose someone set the fire for that reason, do you?"

"Whatever do you mean?"

"To get rid of Mary's things?"

"My goodness, what an imagination you have. Why on earth would anyone want to do that?"

"I don't know." Jennie chewed on her lower lip.

The duchess set her cup and saucer on the tray. "I'm feeling very tired."

"I'm sorry. Maybe I shouldn't have come."

"Nonsense. I thoroughly enjoyed our visit. You'll have to come again."

"I will." Jennie began picking up the teacups.

The duchess waved her hand. "Leave them. Megan will take care of them."

"I'm not used to being waited on."

"You're a dear girl. Now off with you. I need to rest."

"William said I could explore the castle and that I should tell you so you won't think some stranger is poking around."

"What a wonderful idea, Jennie. Be sure to visit the library. It was Liam's great treasure. We have all the classics."

"I will. Thanks for the tea."

Jennie went straight back to her room, gathered up Mary's diaries, and headed for the main staircase. From there she took the hallway she'd accidently taken that first night. She found the library with no trouble and set the diaries on the huge desk. The desk itself was a work of art, Jennie noticed. Though she didn't know antiques, she knew the desk had to be worth a fortune.

She'd always loved libraries, but this one touched her deep inside. There was something special in this place. It felt familiar, welcoming and warm. Jennie almost felt as if she'd been there before—which of course wasn't possible. Unless . . . maybe Gram had brought her there when they'd visited Ireland all those years ago.

Floor-to-ceiling shelves held what must have been thousands of books. They were catalogued, Jennie noticed as her gaze moved over an oak card file similar to those in public libraries. Had Liam done all this himself? Jennie's admiration for him grew. As she scanned the room, her gaze came to rest on a life-size portrait. Jennie looked up at him, sure she'd seen him before. His wistful smile drew her closer. His name, Liam Kavanagh, had been engraved on a gold nameplate.

"Hey, Liam," she said in a library voice. "Great library you have here."

He seemed to look back at her, pleased with her compliment. Jennie did a double take. *It's a portrait, not a person.* The artist had done a fantastic job. Liam looked real enough to step out of the portrait and have a conversation with her. Jennie sighed, wishing she could have known him, feeling angry because he'd died so young. "So who did it, Liam? Who killed you? Or did you kill yourself? Doesn't seem like you'd do that. William said you had everything going for you. And if you killed yourself, why did someone shoot Mac? Why try to kill Gram and me? Did Mac kill you?"

You've lost it, McGrady. You're talking to a portrait. Jennie shook her head to clear it. Reluctantly she moved away from the portrait. She felt as though she were turning away from something important, yet the feelings she had when she looked directly at him gave her an odd sense of déjà vu.

Jennie perused the shelves, touching the leather and pulling out a title here and there. She found an entire section on theology; books on the history of Ireland; several about the history of the Kavanagh clan and other Irish clans; many books on the Celts. Along with the nonfiction,

Jennie found novels by well-known writers like Hemingway and Fitzgerald. There were newer books as well, and Jennie suspected Declan and William had carried on the tradition.

The books captured Jennie's heart, but not nearly as deeply as Liam's portrait did. She kept sneaking looks at him. Jennie finally gave up and went back to study the portrait in more detail. The oils gave his skin and clothing a realistic texture. Up close, she could see the brush marks. She leaned even closer to read the artist's name, which had been painted in the right-hand corner: *Hugh O'Donnell*.

A thrill of excitement rippled through Jennie. Her great-grandfather had painted it.

No wonder she had been so drawn to the portrait.

He's not your grandfather.

As she backed away, Jennie remembered why the portrait seemed so familiar. The photo of the handsome young man that had been among Mary's photos was of Liam. The angle was slightly different, and the photo was in shades of gray while the portrait had been painted with vibrant colors.

Jennie wondered when Hugh had painted the portrait. The date on the gold plaque had Liam's birth and death dates. His eyes in the portrait were not as innocent as in the photo. There was a tiredness in his eyes and tiny lines around them. Jennie guessed the portrait had been done in Liam's early twenties, which was how old he was when he died. Jennie had a moment's panic. Hugh had been painting his portrait. . . . Could they have fought? They must have been friends for Liam to have contracted the portrait. Could they have become enemies?

Jennie refused to believe that. Any man who could paint a portrait like this had to be a friend, not a man capable of murder. Still, Jennie knew of artists with a dark side.

Eager to learn more, Jennie took Mary's diaries to one of the window seats and settled herself against the cushions. She opened the journal she'd been reading and found where she'd stopped.

On the very next page, Mary talked about Hugh's being commissioned to paint Liam's portrait.

> *I was angry at first. I didn't want him to do it. But then I realized how foolish my anger had been. Hugh teased me about my reaction, but I could soon see that he was hurt. He thought I didn't think he could do it. Of course it wasn't that at all.*

"What was it, then?" Jennie asked aloud.

> *I've resigned myself to it. Not that I am worried. Liam would never confide our dark secret to Hugh or to anyone else. Just as I swore that I would take it to the grave.*

Jennie stopped reading. "Dark secret?" In that instant she knew. The baby's father was Liam. Jennie waited while the shock washed over her. They had been in love at one time. What had happened? Why hadn't they married?

For the same reason Gram and William hadn't become anything more than friends—class and religion. Liam was Anglican. Mary was Catholic. He was rich and she poor.

"How tragic," Jennie murmured.

Hungry for more information, Jennie opened the diary again. Mary talked about how Hugh had gone off to war and how Liam had tried and been rejected because of an old injury to his leg. Mary had gone to work at the castle.

> *I didn't want to, but Liam insisted it was the only practical thing to do. He has been nothing if not the perfect gentleman, but each day I walk with my darling girl up the road to Liam's home, my heart shatters. Liam feels it as well, and I don't doubt that Maude suspects that Liam and I were once more than friends. Perhaps she sees Liam in Helen's eyes—those dark blue penetrating eyes that seem to look right into your soul. I don't think I can bear it much longer.*

The next entry was brief.

The worst imaginable news came today. Hugh has died.

The rest of the book was blank. Jennie then opened the other diary, which she quickly discovered was actually the first. It began the day Mary had gotten the diary as a birthday gift from her little sister, Catherine. Mary had just turned sixteen. The first few pages went on about her life and how she and Liam would walk along the beach.

When Jennie turned to the next page, she discovered a letter addressed to Gram. She felt suddenly guilty for having read the diaries without Gram. She tapped the letter against her cheek. Had Gram come back yet?

Jennie's gaze connected with Liam's once again . . . with his dark eyes. Why hadn't she realized it sooner? This time she saw in his features the child and grandchildren and great-grandchildren he'd helped to bring into the world. Gram, Dad and Kate, Nick and Jennie. Liam Kavanagh, not Hugh O'Donnell, was her great-grandfather. Jennie was a Kavanagh.

Her stomach twisted in fear. The things that had happened to her and Gram since they'd arrived may have had nothing to do with Gram's looking into Liam's death—or with Thomas and the farm. Gram was an heir to the Kavanagh fortune, and she didn't even know it. Jennie wondered now if someone wanted to make certain she never found out.

Jennie's discussion with the duchess suddenly made more sense. What better way to stop them from coming to Ireland with a threat? Then the attack on Gram as she was coming out of the police station, and the fire. Those failed. As did the bombing. The brake line had been meant to kill them, but it had failed too. Mac had sent the note and probably cut the brake line. Had he also set the fire and planted the bomb? But what about his death? Where did that fit in?

What did it mean? If Gram found out who her real

father was, William stood to lose half of everything he'd inherited from his father. Had he taken steps to make certain she didn't?

Jennie's heart nearly stopped. "Gram is with him right now."

23

Where were they? Had William lied about wanting to find out about his father? Jennie's head throbbed with unanswered questions. The only thing she knew for certain was that she and Gram were in danger—more now than ever. If William found out that Jennie knew, he'd kill her for sure.

Calm down, McGrady. Jennie took several slow, deep breaths. *You have to think this through.*

"There you are, Jennie." William opened the door to the library and stepped inside. "What is it? You look white as a sheet."

"Wh-where is Gram?" *You have to play it cool, McGrady. Don't let on that you know anything.*

William frowned and took a step toward her.

Jennie winced. She hadn't meant to. "I need to talk to Gram."

"What's frightened you?" He came closer.

You. Jennie moved out of the window seat so she could run if she needed to. "I'm not afraid. You startled me is all."

"I'm sorry. Thought you might want to hear the news."

"What's that?"

"We've gotten Thomas out of jail."

"Great." She managed a smile.

"Yes, poor chap." His gaze moved to his father's portrait. "Have you been enjoying our library? My father put much of it together himself, you know. Inherited some from our ancestors, of course, and Declan and I have added volumes over the years. But the bulk of it was his."

"It's beautiful." *What have you done with Gram?* She wanted to ask but was afraid of what his answer might be. Had he killed Gram and come after her?

"Helen's father painted his portrait, you know."

"I . . . I saw that." Jennie frowned. *He doesn't know.* Jennie wasn't certain how she had come to that conclusion, but she all of a sudden realized that William had no idea that he and Gram had the same father. "Where did you say Gram was?"

"Having tea with the duchess. Thought you might like to join us."

Jennie relaxed some. William was no more a killer than she was. *Which leaves Declan.* That made more sense. Declan was the one in charge of the financial empire. He ran the castle. He'd asked them to stay at the castle. Had he meant to scare them away at first? Declan could easily have gotten Mac to do his dirty work for him. She glanced at her watch. Three-thirty.

Hadn't Declan said he'd be back around three?

"Is Declan here?" she asked.

"Not that I know of. He should be along any moment. Are you anxious to go riding?"

Jennie shrugged. "Not especially." Jennie had no intention of going anywhere with Declan. Not now. She had to let Gram know what she'd discovered. But how? And Jennie had no idea how William would react once he knew. *You only have one option*, Jennie decided. *Go to tea and take Gram aside to tell her what you've learned.* She just hoped Declan didn't show up before she had the chance.

When Jennie walked into the room, her intuition sparked like a live electrical wire. The hairs on the back of her neck rose to attention, alerting her to some sort of danger. But why? *What could possibly be wrong?*

Gram sat in a straight-backed chair next to Maude's

chaise lounge. She looked relaxed. So did the duchess. They stopped talking when Jennie and William came in.

"I thought you were going riding." Gram put her teacup aside.

"Would you like some tea, dear?" the duchess asked.

"I need to talk to Gram."

"Can't it wait until we've had our tea?" The duchess seemed distressed at the interruption.

"Um . . . sure, I guess." Jennie wondered how the duchess would feel about Gram's being a stepdaughter. It would be awkward, but she seemed the unsinkable type. She'd probably laugh and welcome them into the family.

The duchess's hand shook as she poured Jennie a cup. Jennie took it and sat down on the floor next to Gram.

Gram dropped her cup and grabbed the arm of the chair. "I—" Grasping her stomach, she toppled out of the chair.

Jennie dropped to her knees. "Gram! What's wrong?" Looking up at William, she cried, "Call an ambulance! Hurry."

Gram was doubled over, writhing in pain. She clutched at Jennie's arm. "Poison. Get . . . out."

The world shifted into slow motion. Jennie couldn't have heard right. *Poison?*

She glanced at the duchess, who'd turned pasty white.

"Who did it? Who poisoned you?"

Gram didn't answer.

William stared at Gram, his mouth open. Then he seemed to come to himself. "I'll call . . ." He hurried out of the room.

In that moment Jennie knew the horrid truth. It wasn't William or Declan who had tried to kill them. It had been the duchess. Now it all made sense. She wanted them dead but needed someone she could trust—Mac. Then, to keep him from talking, she'd killed him. Mac had written the note to warn Gram.

"You." Jennie rose to her knees.

"Your grandmother and I were having the most interesting conversation," Maude said. She slurred her words, and Jennie wondered if she'd been drinking something other than tea.

"I was telling her I hoped it wouldn't come to this. You see, I did my best to simply frighten the two of you away. Nothing worked."

Jennie rose and took a step toward her.

"Stay where you are." Maude drew a small gun from the folds of her skirt and pointed it at Jennie. "My dear girl, I'm afraid you know too much. You'll have to die too."

"No . . ." Gram tried to stand up. She lunged at the duchess. "Let her go. She doesn't know." Gram fell to the floor at Maude's feet.

"You've killed her." Jennie swallowed back her rising fear.

"Yes. It's much less messy than a gunshot, but you've given me no choice." Maude raised the gun again, her hand shaking. Jennie dove to the floor as the gun went off.

24

Jennie scrambled to her feet and lunged at the old woman, knocking over the table and the chair in which she'd been sitting. Jennie landed on top of her, wrenched the gun away, and rolled off.

William, Jeremy, and Declan ran in.

"Stay right there." Jennie backed against the wall, holding the gun on them. She didn't know whom to trust or what to do. Her gaze went to Gram, who lay far too still.

Declan's gaze shot from Jennie and the gun to Gram and the duchess. "What in blazes have you done?"

"She's made a mess of things, that's what," Maude said. "I did it for you. For all of you."

"What is she talking about?" Declan took a step toward Jennie. "Give me the gun."

"N-no." Jennie's hands were shaking now too. "Gram's been poisoned." Her words collapsed in a rush of tears. "Please help her."

Declan took advantage of the opportunity and grabbed Jennie, pulling the gun out of her grasp.

"Please don't kill us," Jennie pleaded. "I won't tell anyone. You can have your money. Just get an ambulance."

"I already did," William said.

"Jeremy," Declan said, "you'd better phone the police as well. Looks like it's going to take a while to sort things out here."

William cradled Gram in his arms. "She's alive."

Jennie stumbled over to her grandmother and dropped down beside her. She wiped her eyes with her hands. *This is no time to fall apart, McGrady. You have to keep it together for Gram.*

Gram's breathing was shallow, her pulse slow.

Jennie prayed.

Declan knelt beside his grandmother on the chaise. "Hold on, Duchess," he pleaded.

The duchess closed her eyes. "There's a letter," she gasped. "For William."

Jennie came up behind Declan. "I didn't mean to hurt her. She was going to shoot me. She killed Mac and poisoned Gram. She was going to kill me too."

Sirens screamed. Jennie could see the lights as they sped up the drive.

"We can sort it all out later." Declan stood. "Jeremy, go let them in."

A moment later the medics rushed into the room and within seconds had Gram on a stretcher. One of them was hooking up an IV while another went to work on Maude.

They spent several minutes working on the old woman. Finally one of the medics turned away from her and settled a hand on Declan's shoulder. "She's dead. I'm sorry."

Declan nodded. Jennie covered her mouth to hold in anguished sobs.

"Come on." Declan ushered Jennie and Jeremy out of the room.

"I'm going to the hospital with Helen." William's tone brooked no argument. "Jennie will come with me."

"She'll need to talk to the inspector," Declan said.

"She will. We all will. He can find us at the hospital." William guided Jennie down the stairs.

"Then Jeremy and I will come as well. I need some answers myself."

On the way to the hospital, Jennie told them about Mary and Liam. "Liam was Gram's father."

Tears gathered in William's eyes, but he didn't seem

too surprised. "I always knew there was something tying us together. Funny, as a lad I imagined she was my sister. I wish I'd known."

"I thought you did. I was afraid you'd been trying to get rid of us."

"Oh, Jennie. Never. I love your grandmother with all my heart." He paused. "Now I understand why."

At the hospital, the doctors confirmed that Gram had been poisoned with arsenic. They'd pumped her stomach and said she was very lucky to be alive. The duchess had ingested the poison as well, but her condition had been exacerbated by a heart attack and old age.

Something happened to Jennie during the few days she sat in the hospital with Gram. She'd done a lot of thinking about a lot of things. One was that she wondered about her career choice. She'd been so set on going into law enforcement, but now she wasn't so sure. Maybe it was something her cousins had said the day of the picnic about her making a good doctor. As she watched the doctors and nurses helping this patient and that, Jennie wondered what it might be like to go into medicine. That would certainly make her mother happy. Jennie decided not to say anything yet. She needed to think on it awhile.

She'd also done a lot of thinking about Ryan and decided that, as soon as she got home, she'd call him. Seeing him face-to-face would answer a lot of questions.

The duchess was buried in the cemetery at the Anglican church, next to Liam's grave.

After the funeral Gram and William gathered everyone in the library at the castle. "We have some ghosts to put to rest," Gram said.

Jennie headed for the window seat, where she'd been reading Mary's diaries. They were gone now. Gram had

them and had shared them with William. The others—
Gram, William, Declan, and Jeremy—had settled into the
mahogany leather chairs.

"I'd like to begin with an apology," William said. "Had
I not insisted that Helen help me to discover what had
happened to my father, I doubt any of this would have
happened."

Gram reached a hand out to him and he took it. "You
mustn't blame yourself."

"I didn't think Liam's death had anything to do with
it," Jennie said. "Didn't Maude just want to get rid of you
so you wouldn't find out that Liam was your father?" Jennie had a lot of questions about Maude. Bitterness and
greed had turned her into a cold-blooded killer.

"Yes, but I think there was more to it than that." Gram
released William's hand and stood, beginning to pace as
she spoke. "Maude had a lot to say to me when she invited
me for tea. She began by telling me that Liam was my
father." She ran a hand through her hair. "I was shocked,
to say the least. With Maude's confession, the diaries, and
the letters—William's from Maude and mine from Mary—
we've been able to piece together what happened."

"It began when they were children." William gazed at
Gram with a sad smile. "Liam's parents forbade him to
have anything to do with Mary."

"Because she was Catholic and poor." Jennie tucked
her feet under her. The discrimination saddened her.

"Yes. The O'Donnells were farmers—commoners,"
William answered. "Apparently the love Liam and Mary
had for one another transcended those boundaries."

"Must seem kind of strange that you and William went
through the same thing," Jennie said to Gram, shifting so
she sat sideways in the window, with her back against the
frame.

"In a way." William nodded. "But Helen and I were
never in love. We adored each other, much as a sister and
brother would."

"Which is what you were."

"Aye," William said. "Perhaps that explains why both our families tried so hard to keep us apart. But enough about us. Let's get back to Mary and Liam." William went on to tell the group how Mary and Liam had fallen in love as teenagers and vowed that, despite their differences, they would someday marry. And they did. Liam and Mary ran away together. Liam pretended to be Catholic, and they married in Dublin, where no one knew them. After a brief honeymoon there, they returned home to two sets of outraged parents.

The parents entered into a pact. The marriage would be annulled, and neither family would ever speak of it again. It was over. Mary was sent off to Galway to work for a friend of the family. Liam was sent to England to a private school—a military academy. He returned home and discovered his love married to Hugh O'Donnell and expecting a child. A broken man by then, Liam married the woman his father had chosen.

"So they really were married." Jennie felt relieved at that. "Why didn't the church records show it? On the copies I got, it looked like someone had changed them."

"I don't know," Gram said. "Perhaps the parents had them altered. Or perhaps Maude hired someone to do it. It's one of those things we may never know.

"It could have been either," Gram went on. "Maude had no idea about Liam's first and only love until Hugh went off to war and Liam hired Mary to work in the castle. It didn't take long for Maude to figure out what had happened. When Hugh died, she feared that Liam would divorce her and remarry his first love. She talked with Mary and was assured that Mary would never be instrumental in breaking up the marriage. Maude had nothing to fear. Mary left the castle, and a few years later Liam was dead."

"Did Maude kill him?" Jennie asked.

"We're not sure of that," Gram said. "He was certainly

202

despondent. After Mary left, his depression worsened."

Jeremy, who'd been silent to that point, said, "I still don't understand why the duchess tried to kill Jennie and Helen. How could she do all that stuff?"

"She didn't," Gram answered. "Maude somehow got Mac to come at me with that van. The police uncovered it, by the way. No fingerprints, but they expect to find evidence that he had driven it. It belonged to a farmer east of here. It was Mac who set fire to the house and who cut the brake line."

"Did he plant the bomb too?" Jennie leaned back against the cool window.

"No," William answered. "We've determined that the bombing was something else altogether. It was the same group responsible for the other bombings in the area."

"What about Mac?" Jennie glanced down at the outbuildings, then back to the others. "She had to have killed him."

"Yes." Gram frowned. "We suspect that Mac refused to do anything more and may have threatened to talk to the police."

"Such a waste." Declan stood and stretched. "I suppose one good thing has come of all of this."

"What's that?" William asked.

"Jeremy has a cousin." He nodded at Jennie. "Now he has someone to stay with when he visits the States."

Jeremy perked up. "I hadn't thought of that."

"I've spoken with Jennie's parents, and they said they'd be happy to have you any time."

"Are you trying to get rid of me?"

"Actually, I thought we'd visit the States together. I'd like to spend some time with my cousins as well. I know how badly you've been wanting to go. If you're so inclined, you can stay a bit longer."

Jennie grinned at Jeremy and was already thinking of things they could do together.

The next morning Jennie and Gram hiked down the beach to the farm. Just as they reached the house, a mini-van turned into the drive.

"I wonder who that is." Jennie peered at the occupants, but they were still too far away.

"Shall we go see?"

She raced into the yard just as the doors opened. Nick jumped down and flew into Jennie's arms, nearly knocking her over. Lisa emerged then, opening her arms wide to give Jennie a hug. Mom and Dad joined in the flurry, with everybody hugging everybody else.

"My daughter the detective. Can't let you out of my sight for a minute, can I?" Dad settled an arm around her shoulders and pulled her toward him.

"I don't think you have to worry about that anymore, Dad."

"What do you mean?"

"Would you be too disappointed if I decided to go into medicine instead of law?"

He grinned down at her. "Disappointed? I'd be thrilled. So would your mother."

"Well, don't say anything yet, but I'm thinking about it."

"Thanking about what?" Mom came around the car and enveloped her in a hug.

"I'll tell you later." Jennie stepped back. "What are you doing here? I didn't think you were coming till next week."

"We wanted to surprise you," Mom said. "We'd planned it all along."

"It's a surprise, all right."

Jennie was just setting Nick down when she saw him. He was taller that she remembered. His hair was lighter and his eyes bluer. Butterflies fluttered around in her stomach and set her heart to thumping.

"Hi, Jennie." He took a tentative step toward her.

So this was the surprise. "Ryan, hi." Jennie stood there a minute, not sure what to say. She didn't even know how she felt. Good, she decided. Definitely good. She wasn't as upset with him as she thought she'd be. Still, she hadn't altogether forgiven him either. As their gazes locked, the months they'd been apart seemed to melt away. She'd give him another chance.

"I hope you don't mind my coming. Your folks said it would be okay, and Gram paid for my ticket. . . ."

"I'm glad you came." Jennie reminded herself to breathe. She grinned because she couldn't help it and watched him walk toward her. As he did, she wondered two things: first, how it would feel to kiss him after all these months; and second, how he would like Shelagh's special cookies.

brio girls

REAL Faith MEETS REAL Life

Tackling issues of faith, family, friendship, dating, and more, these *Brio Girls* books are the stories of real-life teens struggling to make the right choices and learning to see the consequences of all their decisions, both good and bad. These books hit the mark on what life is like today.

1. Stuck in the Sky

Jacie's confused about life and feels guilty for not sharing her faith more. Can she find a unique way to share her love of God with others?

2. Fast Forward to Normal

Becca just wants life to return to the way it was. When it doesn't, will she do what God asks of her?

3. Opportunity Knocks Twice

Tyler's torn between two girls, and deciding between them means following God or going his own way. Which will he choose?

4. Double Exposure

A whirlwind ski trip finds Hannah kissing two boys! Can she return to a courtship lifestyle...and does she want to?

BETHANYHOUSE

11400 Hampshire Ave. S., Minneapolis, MN 55438
www.bethanyhouse.com • (800) 328-6109